Outback Sunrise

ANNIE SEATON

Richards Brothers: Book 3

Dedication

This book is dedicated to all my grey nomie readers who travel this wonderful land of ours. I hope you enjoy the little glimpse of the Northern Territory.

Chapter One

Jessica Trent walked slowly between the rows of rental cars looking for the small red sedan described on the rental contract she clutched in her hand. The other hand had a firm grip on the handle of the leopard print suitcase that clattered along behind her. Her matching carry-on bag was perched precariously on top of the suitcase, and threatened to fall as it bumped against the laptop bag jammed underneath it.

"At last." She sighed with relief when she spotted the vehicle at the end of the row and stepped out briskly, relieved to finally deposit her luggage. The heat in the strong wind blowing across the tarmac was unbelievable, and the light silk of her skirt and long-sleeved jacket stuck uncomfortably to her damp skin. She unlocked the car, stowed her luggage in the trunk, slipped into the driver's seat, and turned the air conditioning up to top speed.

Pulling out her mobile, she switched it on, and an Australian service provider appeared almost instantly. She hit the speed dial for Monica's number, and then realised she had to put the international code prefix before the mobile number and she didn't have a clue what it was. All those details were stored in her laptop computer now buried in the trunk.

"Shit." Reaching down she searched for the lever to pop the trunk down and caught her fingernail beneath the hard plastic edge.

"Double shit." She examined her once perfectly manicured long red fingernails and glared at the broken nail of her index finger. Lack of sleep on the flight over had left her out of sorts. She took a deep breath before she opened the door. Heat blasted into the car, instantly dissipating the cool air from the air conditioning. She scurried around to the rear of the car and retrieved the laptop from behind the large suitcase. A strong gust of hot wind caught the door above her head and slammed it down onto her shoulders just as she straightened.

"Ouch." So far Australia wasn't doing much for her.

She backed out and slammed the door down. When she was back in the car, she reached up to her shoulder and groaned when her hand came away from her silk blouse that was now covered in grease. No way was she getting her suitcase out again to change. She would get to her destination first. And anyway, it was way too hot to get out of the car.

Firing up the laptop, she scrolled through her contacts and found the international prefix she had stored in her address book and entered the digits onto the touch screen of her phone.

"Come on, Mon. Pick up." The phone rang continuously and Jess could feel her temper rising when her best friend didn't pick up straight away. "Please," she muttered, drumming her fingers on the steering wheel. Finally, the call connected and she heaved a sigh of relief when Monica answered.

"Do you know what time it is, Jess?"

"Oh sorry, I forgot about the time difference."

"I suppose that means you've landed and you're down under safely."

"Yes, I've just arrived in Darwin. Has Gareth found a hotel for me?"

"He's working late tonight. There's a big campaign coming up and he has to go back to the UK for a photo shoot next week so he sent me an email from the office. I forwarded it to you before I went to bed. It's got the name of the closest town to the resort."

"Oh, thank goodness. I didn't know whether to book into a hotel here or drive straight to Cockatoo Springs."

"Have you looked at a map yet, Jess? I know what you're like. You'll drive off without even checking that you're even on the right freeway.

Daly River is the closest town to the resort and there should be a couple of hotels there. I'll e-mail you some links before I go back to bed."

"I'll be fine, so stop worrying. Now that I know where to go, I can put it into the GPS and head off."

"Worrying?"

Jess held the phone away from her ear, prepared for Monica's rant as her friend's voice hit squeal pitch. Gazing through the window, she watched the palm trees across the tarmac bend in the strong wind. They had flown over a large bay just before the aircraft touched down and the screen on the back of the seat in front of her displayed the name Fannie Bay. It was a shame she couldn't spend more time here before she headed into the outback. The morning sunlight had glinted invitingly off the sapphire blue water and a line of resorts and sailboats had edged the coastline. Now it was late morning and high thunderclouds were building over the sea, and it looked like a tropical storm was on the way.

"Are you listening to me?" Monica's voice was getting louder with each word.

"Yes, I'm listening."

"Well, as soon as you get there safely, call me. Gareth said as long as you have the application in by the end of the month, you'll be fine. He heard through the grapevine that they aren't interviewing for the new position for a couple of weeks."

"How thoughtful of them. Just in time for Christmas." She glanced down at her watch. She did the quick time calculation and realised it was only eleven o'clock the night before in New York. "Go back to bed, hon. You've got the whole night ahead to sleep, and don't worry about me. I'm determined to get this job. And you know me, I never give up until I get what I want." She ended the call and leaned back on the seat, closing her eyes.

Two weeks. She had two weeks to track down the elusive wonder boy who'd created the innovative bush tucker chef school at Cockatoo Springs resort, and made it a worldwide phenomenon in less than a year. Then get an interview with him and write the best damned article she had ever written about this unique establishment that chefs from all over the world were clamouring to get into. Once the article was subbed, the interview for the fulltime job coming up at *Cuisine* magazine would be in the bag. The job would be hers; she just knew it. It had to be. Since she'd bought her apartment, she couldn't afford to just walk away from the PR job she hated. Working for media magnate, Larry Bartholomew was not what she wanted to do with her journalism degree. It was her off-the-cuff freelance interviews that always ended up as her most successful pieces, but it had been over a year since she had last produced the article that resulted in mega sales for the Christmas issue of *Cuisine* magazine. Once she got the permanent job at the magazine she would enjoy giving in her notice to sleaze ball, Larry. But no matter how bad things got there was no way she was going to run begging to her father for help, even if it meant losing the new little apartment she loved. She'd done her journalism degree, she'd written some fabulous freelance articles and now she was determined to prove to herself she could be a top food journalist.

And prove it to my him. She was already well on the way to proving to her father she could stand on her own two feet. There was no way she was going to run back to him to access her trust fund. He'd be lucky if she ever spoke to him again after the way he'd treated her last year.

Jess opened her eyes and looked down, surprised to see her hands clenched in her lap and she took in a deep breath as the cool air from the air conditioning unit fanned across her hot cheeks and restored a measure of her calm.

Food journalists had been trying to get a feature interview with this guy for the last six months, ever since the outback cuisine trend had hit the top restaurants of New York and Europe. No one had been successful getting an interview, and there wasn't even a photo of him anywhere but she had done her research.

Alessandro Gabrielle Ricardo. I am going to track you down and write the best damn article I can

Jess reached for her phone again, connecting it to her laptop so she could collect her email. Scrolling through, she quickly located Monica's message.

Daly River. The Banyan Tree caravan park.

She reached over and entered Daly River into the GPS.

Two hundred and nineteen kilometres south of the airport displayed on the screen. Doing a quick conversion to miles, she calculated she could do that in less than four hours and would be there well before dark. She slipped her sunglasses down, started the car, and turned right toward the boom gates at the exit. A horn blared in front of her and she quickly angled the car to the other side of the road when she remembered they drove on the left in Australia. She barely missed the silver Mercedes and smiled apologetically at the driver when he glared at her through his window. Turning onto the access road to the international airport, she followed the instructions of the robotic female voice of the GPS, concentrating on staying on the left-hand side of the road. She breathed a sigh of relief when she turned the small sedan onto the on-ramp of the Stuart Highway, set the cruise control, and relaxed into the drive. Thoughts scurried through her mind as she devised and discarded strategies for meeting the mysterious Mr. Ricardo.

She'd overcome the first hurdle and was on her way down the highway to her destination…or close to it. She would book into the resort as a guest, but first would stay in the small town close by to the resort and then do an exploratory foray. Maybe they were hiring kitchen hands or waitresses and she could go in undercover and check him out. This could be exciting and a bit of fun…she thrived on a challenge and her investigative radar twitched.

Finding him and getting the interview would be her two biggest hurdles.

Three hours, and well over one hundred miles later, Jess approached a sign indicating the turn off to Daly River was two kilometres ahead. Even though it was only mid-afternoon, the sky was dark and huge thunderclouds were building in the sky as the storm had followed her down the freeway. The drive on the Stuart Highway had been slow, and she'd passed so many motor homes she'd lost count. She'd driven without a break, sipping on the bottled water she'd bought at the airport. Jet lag finally caught up with her and she turned off the freeway and followed the narrow, winding road to Daly River for another hour. The bitumen road ended, and just as she began to worry she'd taken the wrong turn, she crested a hill and a sign with

Daly River, three kilometres, appeared.

Five minutes later, a small caravan park with a vacancy sign out front was the only sign of life amongst the short scrubby trees. She drove along the road until she came to a closed-up brick building with a police sign hanging crookedly out front, and then the road came to a dead end at a wide river. Turning the car around, Jess drove back to the caravan park to a timber building that had 'reception' written across the front window. She stepped out of the car just as the sky broke and large raindrops splattered on her silk suit. By the time she'd pushed open the door of the small office, it was pouring and rivulets of water were running across the driveway.

The woman at the desk looked up as the bell above the door rang. She reached under the counter, brought out a handful of paper towels and passed them to Jess. "Looks like you got a bit damp, darl."

"Thank you," Jess said, mopping at the sodden silk. "At least it's a bit cooler now."

"Bit of a worry when the heavy rains come this quick, though," said the older woman. "Early start to the wet season. Are you after a cabin or just shopping?" She smiled and looked Jess up and down, obviously taking in the suit and the Jimmy Choos.

"I was looking for Daly River. Have I taken the wrong turn?"

"Nope, you've found us, love. We are Daly River. Since the police station closed and the river cut the road to the other caravan park, we're it." She looked at Jess, curiosity filling her face. "So, why Daly River? You don't look like you're here for the fishing."

"I was hoping to get a room…or a cabin here for the one night. You do have vacancy?"

"I've only got one cabin left down the back near the river. The fishing season has started and the park is full."

"That will do nicely." Jess smiled and she scrabbled in her handbag for her wallet. The bell rang again as the glass door pushed open and a deep voice rumbled behind her.

"Are you the idiot driver who has blocked the loading bay?"

Jess jumped and dropped her wallet. Before she bent to pick it up, she drew herself to her full height, under six foot in her heels, and let the ice drip from her voice.

"Excuse me?"

"Ha…should have known it. A bloody Yank." The owner of the voice towered over her. "No idea about outback road courtesy."

Jess curled her nose as an unpleasant aroma pervaded her nostrils, and she put her hand over her mouth. She looked him up and down, not at all intimidated by the glowering look on the face of this…this person. Long legs encased in stained jeans, a tight black T-shirt moulding a broad chest, and a deeply tanned, unshaven face with shaggy black hair pulled back and tied at the nape of his neck with what looked like a dirty piece of string which trailed over one shoulder.

"What is that dreadful smell?" She bent to retrieve her wallet and kept one hand across her mouth.

"Live bait for crabs. Prawn, mullet and herring burley." He put his heads on his hips as she stood. "Look, love, I've got a load of barra to put into the cool room out here. It's sitting out in my truck in the heat and your bloody car is blocking the way, so if I ask nicely would you go out and move it?"

"Since you have been so polite, I will move it as soon as I check in." She hadn't understood a word he'd said about the smell and the accent didn't help either. Placing her keys and wallet on the counter, she turned to the woman who was watching the exchange with a broad grin on her face.

"May I have the check-in form, please?" She gasped as a large tanned hand whipped past her arm and grabbed her keys.

"What the hell do you think you're doing?" Jess tried to keep her voice level as he dangled the keys rudely in front of her face.

"I'll move the car for you. Janet here will get you all checked in," he said. "Which cabin, Janet?" He turned to the woman behind the counter. "I may as well park it for the sweet young lady."

Jess was at a loss for words. No way did she want this unkempt hulk knowing her room number.

"Last one on the left down by the boat ramp," Janet called after him as he strode to the door. "And watch out for the crocodile. There's been a biggie hanging around the ramp all day. The rain might get him wandering."

"Oh, and by the way." He paused in the doorway and looked back over one shoulder." Don't look at me as though I've just crawled out of the slime. The back of *your* pretty shirt is covered in grease." The door slammed shut behind him

Jess looked up at the woman behind the counter. "Are all Australian men so…so rude?"

"Nah, don't worry about Alex, he was in a rush. He'll be anxious to get home with the rain coming and he has a heap of fish to cool down. The season has just started."

Home? He looked like he belonged in a cabin in the wilds, and what's more he smelled like it.

Jess completed the check-in, picked up the door key, and stomped through the rain down to the back of the small park, and retrieved her keys from the rental car. She was relieved to see no sign of the smelly truck driver hanging about her room. Standing at the door of the cabin, she put the key in the lock of the flimsy door, pulling at her suit with her other hand. It was sodden, and sticking to her underwear. Water splashed as a black pick-up truck, loaded with blue crates, sped down the road past her cabin and slowed when it got to her car.

"And sweetheart, you can see right through the front of your suit. Nice view, though. Like the lace G-string." He laughed, gunned the engine, and took off. Mud splashed the front of her skirt and legs before she had a chance to reply.

Jess stepped out onto the road and gave him the finger.

Not the best reply, but satisfying.

Chapter Two

Alex Richards turned on to Cox's Road down past the conservation area. He'd probably been a bit tough on the woman, but she'd really annoyed him and he was in a tearing hurry.

If this rain didn't stop, the river would be up and he'd have to take the long route back to Cockatoo Springs and offload the fish before he left. He gunned the motor and the pickup fishtailed down the narrow road. The wet wasn't due for another fortnight and he'd misjudged the weather forecast and left his run too late. Even though he'd been in the Northern Territory for a couple of years, he still couldn't predict the weather with any accuracy. He'd missed the damn forecast this morning, and if the creek was up, he wouldn't be able to get the barramundi to the airstrip to be flown in to Cockatoo Springs in time, and it would have to go to Darwin instead. The new chef from London at the resort had specifically requested fresh barramundi as soon as he had his first catch.

The truck crested the hill and he cursed at the sight in front of him. Not only was the river up, it had already broken its banks and had spread into the scrubby trees in the conservation area.

Shit. He slammed his hands on to the steering wheel. It looked like it had been raining upriver for a while before it had hit downstream. The rain had only started here when he'd driven into town an hour ago. He picked up his mobile and made a quick call and organised for the courier truck leaving the next town for the local airstrip, to wait for him at the caravan park so he could transfer the load of fish across from the cool room.

He wasn't looking forward to driving back to the resort the long way. For a moment, he considered going back to Darwin and picking up the helicopter, but then decided if he got an early start in the morning, it would be almost as quick to take the shortcut through the gorge. In the meantime, he'd go back to Janet's and get a cabin for the night, after they'd transferred the barramundi to the truck.

Damn the early rain. It had stuffed up all his plans.

He drove back into Daly River, surprised to see it had already stopped raining. The afternoon sun was slanting through the trees and the sky had cleared from the west. Maybe the river would go down quickly…so long as snere was no more rain. He might be able to take the short route yet. It all depended on whether the rains held off for a few more days.

After loading the refrigerated van and waving

the driver off to the airstrip, he parked his pickup truck out the front of the park.

"Gotta room for me, Janet?" he called through to the kitchen as he waited at the counter. Janet came out wiping her hands on her apron and shook her head. "Sorry, Alex, all full up. The American girl got the last cabin. I think everyone on the road was a bit spooked by the early rain."

That'd be right. Miss America had already messed his day up, now she'd taken the last room.

"I guess I'll have to try the pub over at Douglas River."

Janet shook her head. "No go, I was just talking to Cliff on the phone. They're full over in Douglas too. Listen, the old trailer down the back is empty. If you are happy to shower up here, you can bunk down there. No charge."

Alex reached over and hugged the older woman. "You're a sweetheart. I'll unload and have that shower. That burley *was* extra ripe today."

Janet laughed. "I think poor Miss America was a bit overwhelmed."

"Bloody tourists. They come to the outback; they have to take us as they find us. What's she doing here anyway? She looks like she should be lounging by a pool somewhere.'

"Don't know." Janet shrugged. "She only booked in for the one night."

"Well, she's not my problem," Alex said.

"I've got enough to worry about with this bloody rain coming early. You cooking tonight?" When she nodded, he smiled. "I'll be up for dinner, then."

###

Two hours later, after a shower, a shave, and a quick nap in the trailer, Alex pulled on clean jeans and a fresh black T-shirt and made his way across to the small dining room behind the office. The backdrop of the sky was inky black, and the stars were brilliant white against the darkness. The croaking of frogs was overlaid by the thrum of insects stirred up by the rain. He took a deep breath and inhaled the dewy freshness of the night as he walked across the car park to the dining room.

There was no place like the outback.

The heavy rain had broken the heat and the night was quite pleasant, apart from the mosquitoes that buzzed around his head. Well, it was. Until he walked into the dining room. Miss America, as Janet called her, was the sole occupant of the restaurant, sitting at the bar sipping on a cocktail. Of course, he thought. A cocktail would go with the fancy duds. Obviously not a beer drinker. He nodded briefly to her and allowed a lazy smile to cross his face when recognition dawned.

"Nice evening," he said.

"Very pleasant," she said and turned her back to him to peruse the menu propped on the counter against an old bottle in a basket. Candle wax stuck in splotches to the side of the bottle, and Alex smothered a grin. Probably not the high-class décor this one was used to. He wondered what she was doing in a caravan park in an isolated outpost like Daly River. She looked as though she'd be much more comfortable in the club lounge at Cockatoo Springs.

Janet came through from the kitchen, order pad in hand. "Have you decided, Jess?"

Jess shook her head. "Still looking. Great menu…if you like fish."

So that was her name. She didn't look like a Jess. Even in the old rundown bar of Janet's establishment, she was dressed in something soft and silky that clung to her curves in all the right places, and hinted at a shadow of cleavage. He raised his gaze from her long bare legs, past her full breasts, and up to encounter a frosty stare. He stared back and she was the first to look away.

"What about you, Alex? A beer?"

He nodded and reached for the bottle Janet had pulled from the fridge underneath the bar, and then popped the twist top. The liquid slid down his throat and he started to regain his equilibrium. He sat at the far end of the bar and looked along the counter where Jess was perched on the stool.

"It's quiet in here tonight."

"All the fishos came in early, ate, and went to the recreation room. There's a football game on the big screen," Janet said. "Which way are you headed tomorrow, Alex?"

Janet wiped down the bar top in front of him while she waited for Miss America to review the menu.

"Back to Cockatoo Springs. If the river doesn't drop, I'll have to go the long way through Aboriginal land."

"Rain's stopped, anyway. Maybe it was just a storm?"

Miss America had put the menu down and was following their conversation with interest. Alex lifted his beer and toasted her.

"Hope the weather improves for your holiday here. Staying long?"

Jess picked up her drink and sipped it slowly, observing him without replying. Long dark lashes fanned around her almond-shaped green eyes.

Either the hair or the lashes were cosmetically enhanced.

Her lashes and brow were dark while her hair was honey gold. It tumbled onto her bare shoulders, the brightly patterned silky top held in place by thin straps. Her skin looked like it had never seen the sun. It was almost alabaster white. Tropical sun wouldn't agree with that.

Janet bustled around the bar carrying a tablecloth and flicked it across a small table near the window.

"You're the only two left to feed now. Alex, be a gentleman and apologise to the young lady here. Then you can give her a bit of background. She's headed for Cockatoo as well."

His head snapped up and he caught the slight grin on Janet's face as she picked up the tableware and napkins from the basket in front of him.

What was she up to?

She knew the road was out and she should have shared that fact with Miss America. And besides, all the guests at Cockatoo Springs flew in by helicopter from Darwin, there was no access from this far south unless you went bush. As soon as the tourists booked in, their travel arrangements were made for them. There was something wrong here. Janet winked at him and headed back into the kitchen. He had the distinct feeling he was being set up. Janet had been trying to pair him off with every female who came through Daly River since he had rolled into the park and bought her ex-husband's fishing boat after he'd signed the contract at Cockatoo Springs. She certainly needn't try it with his one.

No way. Not my type at all.

He turned and returned the stare of the American woman before he eased off the stool and walked the few steps to the other end of the bar where she was perched like a tropical bird, her elegant fingers with brightly painted red nails wrapped around her glass. Alex put his beer bottle down on the old chipped counter and held out his hand.

"I suppose an apology *is* in order," he said gruffly.

She put her drink on the counter and turned to face him, still not speaking.

He stood with his hand outstretched and waited. "I was out of line this afternoon. I was rude to you, and I apologise for the mud. I didn't mean to do that." He tried to keep his face serious, although the picture of her standing in the wet, clinging suit giving him the finger was one of the funniest things he had seen for a while. "Honestly."

She reached out and took his hand. Her long, slender fingers fit nicely into his.

"I'm Alex Richards, and you are Jess…?"

"Jessica Trent. And apology accepted." He held her hand a little bit longer before letting it go to reach for his beer. He could do dinner; it wasn't entirely her fault that his day had gone to shit.

His interest was piqued and Alex narrowed his eyes as he looked at her.

Or was she just like the others who turned up at the resort expecting to meet him and get fodder for their trashy magazines? He'd been sucked in too many times before. He knew he was a sucker for a pretty face and Emily wasn't the only one who'd conned him. But he'd hardened up a lot since those gullible days.

He was careful and there was no way any journalist could have tracked him down here to Daly River

"Well, Jess Trent, seeing as we are the only two eating at this fine establishment tonight and—" He threw a glance at Janet "—our hostess only set one table, join me for dinner?" He waited, wondering whether she had a sense of humour.

"I'd be delighted." She wrinkled her nose delicately and smiled at him. "On one condition. Has that barley smell gone?"

"Barley?"

"The fish stuff."

"Oh, the burley." He laughed and assured her it was all gone as Janet came back from the kitchen and nodded with approval when she saw the two of them smiling.

"Okay folks, what'll be? The fish or the fish?"

Jess laughed. "I'll have the fish, I guess.

A ripple of interest flickered through him. He'd play the gentleman and find out what she was doing here. He was very interested in what a beautiful, elegantly-dressed woman was doing in a rundown caravan park in this backwater supposedly on her way to Cockatoo Springs.

If it turned out she was after Alessandro Ricardo, he'd send her on her way from here and make damn well sure she didn't get anywhere near the resort.

***

The soft light in the room hid the tired furnishings and the scuffed floor. Janet had lit the candle on their table and placed a small vase of wildflowers next to it. Jess looked up to meet an intent gaze focused on her face. Piercing blue eyes surrounded by deep lines looked steadily into hers. The smile lines around his mouth and eyes were white against the deep tan of his weathered face. Suddenly flustered, she reached for her glass and sipped. "So, tell me about this wet that you're talking about. What does that mean?"

"We have a wet season up here in the Top End from about November to March." The drawl in his Australian accent fascinated her. She'd barely spoken to any Aussies since she'd stepped off the plane this morning. Although after the long drive down here, she felt like she'd been here for days.

"The Top End?" It sounded like he knew the area pretty well and might be able tell her the best way to get to the resort tomorrow, especially if he was heading that way.

"The top end of the Territory. Top as in north. From Darwin and the islands, to about where we are now, down here at Daly River. I must have heard wrong. I thought Janet said you were going to Cockatoo Springs?"

His frown deepened and he looked at her while he waited for her to reply. It was hard to pick his age—the crinkly lines around his mouth and eyes maybe had more to do with the sun, than his age. The jet-black hair pulled back into a short ponytail at his nape seemed to be more for convenience than a fashion statement. He wore a faded pair of jeans and a plain black T-shirt, although they were cleaner than the set he'd worn this afternoon. Even though he'd shaved and looked groomed tonight, he still had a rugged, mountain man thing going on.

She tipped her head to the side, trying to decide how much to tell him. Sure, she wanted to get information from him, if he knew the area, but she didn't want to tell him too much. The roads around here seemed pretty isolated and she didn't know him or who he was. Mon had read her the riot act at JFK before her flight. But she'd never see this guy again, so there was no need to tell him the real reason for her sudden visit to the outback.

She leaned forward and lowered her voice despite them being the only customers in the restaurant. Janet was banging pans out in the kitchen.

"Can you keep a secret?"

He nodded slowly and held her gaze with

those piercing blue eyes, and a small frisson of guilt ran up her spine.

"I'm an actress and I've come over here for a rest. I heard Cockatoo Springs was a private resort where you can get back to nature, and I want some time away from the … ah… artifice of Hollywood."

"Interesting." He seemed decidedly unimpressed. "Been in any movies I would have seen? You don't look familiar."

"Probably not. My…er…agent…is building my portfolio and we're very selective about what I take on."

"But you're already needing a total rest?" He put his head to one side and smiled, the smooth lines of his face softening.

"Yes, but I prefer not talk about it. So, what do you do?"

His eyes narrowed, and for a moment she had the distinct feeling they were both playing at the same game.

"I work out of Cockatoo Springs," he said. "I catch the fish and the crabs for the restaurant."

"Oh, how good is that?" she said enthusiastically. "You can tell me the best way to get there."

"The best way?" He leaned forward and propped his chin in his hand, and stared at her. "Didn't the booking agent make a travel plan for you when you booked in?"

"I haven't booked in yet. I decided to drive there myself. I'm used to driving. I ...er... often drive from New York to LA for my work."

"So, you're on Broadway, too?" He looked at her and a huge smile crossed his face. He really was a looker, his white teeth contrasted with his tanned skin and blue eyes.

"What would be so funny about that?" She could feel the scowl crossing her face.

"Nothing," he said. "I'm just impressed. I haven't met any actresses before." He sat back and sipped his beer. "I'll have to make sure I get your autograph."

"Certainly."

The kitchen door pushed open with a clatter. Janet carried across two plates of food and placed them on the table in front of them. Jess drew in a startled breath as all thoughts of acting and Cockatoo Springs flew from her mind. She reached down, grabbed her phone from her bag, and leaned back in her chair framing the plate of food in the grid of the small screen of her iPhone camera.

She totally forgot about the man sitting across from her as she snapped six shots of the meal in front of her, from a variety of angles. She looked up at Alex, suddenly realising he was watching her with a suspicious expression on his face.

"Why are you taking a photo of your dinner?"

Get out of this one, Jess.

Monica had warned her about being careful. There'd been some pretty awful things happen in the outback; she'd seen the movies, read the news, and Monica had read her the riot act at JFK.

"First, Jess…don't tell everyone your life story in the first five minutes." Jess had rolled her eyes. "And second, don't be so trusting. There are scary people out there. Remember that movie we saw about the outback? 'Wolf Creek', I think it was called. "

. Okay, she'd done some theatre classes in college and a little bit of embroidering the truth wouldn't hurt. She'd had plenty of practice fudging her true identity at college and at the office, finding out the hard way that as soon as anyone found out she came from a wealthy, famous family, they looked at her differently. It was all about what they could get from her and not about true friendship. Monica had been the one exception and they'd stayed friends since high school.

After all, she'd never see this dude again. And if anything, she owed him one for the mud splatter this afternoon

"It's my first meal in Australia and I want to remember it," she said weakly.

So much for decent acting.

"An interesting habit," he said. "Although I

agree, Janet's meals are spectacular. She's wasted in a place like this. It never gets very busy, and she does to like to impress the guests."

Jess was barely listening to him. She had speared a piece of fish and raised it reverently to her mouth. She closed her eyes, savouring the taste, and trying to figure out the herbs that combined to give it the subtle flavour. She opened her eyes and that direct blue gaze was fixed on her lips as she chewed delicately. Pointing her fork at him, she pulled out her best imitation of her mother's voice.

"Has anyone never taught you manners? It is extremely rude to stare. Particularly when one is eating."

"You really are a case, aren't you?" Alex threw back his head and laughed. "When 'one' is eating? I think that 'rest' at Cockatoo Springs will do 'one' the world of good."

"Don't be smart. I'm just enjoying my meal. And I like to cook so I am figuring out what is in it."

"Unless you know your bush tucker you won't figure it out." Picking up his fork, he speared a piece of fish and chewed it without taking his gaze from hers. "Lemon myrtle and pepper berries."

"Bush tucker? What's that?" Although she well knew what it was from her research, she was curious to see if he knew much about the local food. And as well as the amazing article on Alessandro she could do another article using this guy; in fact she could do a whole series on the outback.

From the river to the resort. He was an interesting character and would certainly provide some eye candy on the glossy pages against the photographs of the bush tucker dishes. He could lean in front of that black truck of his and hold one of his big fish up for the camera…and flex his muscles. Maybe they could find a good patch of water for the background of the shot Her thoughts wandered away and she starting framing some words around the picture in her head. She looked up as his deep voice interrupted her thoughts.

"Any native flora or fauna used for cooking or medicinal purposes," he said. "It's a popular type of cooking up here in the Territory." She looked at him, her curiosity growing when he explained how the local bush tucker had become an international success.

"Cockatoo Springs has just made the papers. It took out first place in an international competition run by some flash magazine," he said with a hint of pride in his voice. "First out of the top fifty restaurants in the world this year."

Jess's head flew up when he mentioned the competition. It had been the catalyst for her trip— *Cuisine* had run it and that's where she'd first heard about the wealthy guy who'd made it an international success in less than two years. She took a deep breath and choked, trying not to spray him with food. A piece of wild rice lodged in her throat. She placed her hand over her mouth and coughed trying to dislodge it, until the tears ran down her face. She looked up gratefully when Alex handed her a glass of water.

"Thank you." She picked up the paper napkin and dabbed around her chin in case any food had escaped.

Alex leaned back in the chair and watched her wipe her eyes. Unease prickled down her back as guilt filled her. She hated lying, she'd seen enough of that from her father.

"Alex, I was not quite truthful before. I was being careful…because… you know…well…you never know who you meet in the outback."

"That's a wise way to be out here. It's rough country with some odd characters."

A wave of heat rose from her neck and she knew her face would be flaming red, thanks to her pale complexion. He was well spoken, and she decided to come clean. "I don't want you to think I'm taking advantage of you. I'm not really an actress. I'm actually here for my job or that is for a job I am trying to get."

He leaned forward to eat his meal and tipped his head to the side waiting for her to continue. Jess took a deep breath and waited until he had started to chew.

"I'm going out to Cockatoo Springs to do an article on the chef school and interview Alessandro Ricardo, the managing director. You seem to know a lot about bush cuisine, so it would be an interesting angle if I could use you in another article. You could tell me all about the fish, how you catch it, and where it goes." She spoke quickly, encouraged by the intense interest in his expression." I could even do a section on your business, all good publicity for you. Maybe take some photos?"

Now it was his turn to choke on his food. It must be those tiny pieces of rice…or the hot berries on the fish. Clearing his throat, he sat back and observed her for a moment without speaking, and frown lines creased his forehead.

"Hmm. That sounds interesting. No one has ever asked me about the barramundi fishing before. They've not really found it very interesting. Apart from the fishing tourists, that is, certainly not from a cooking angle." He nodded slowly. "I suppose it could help my business."

Jess was surprised to hear a snort from the bar, and she looked up as Janet hurried back into the kitchen.

"Now tell me, how do you intend to get to Cockatoo Springs?" he said with his arms folded across his chest.

"I'm going to drive there in the morning." A

feeling of unease wound its way from her stomach to her chest, and it had nothing to do with the fish she had just eaten.

"You're going to drive three hundred kilometres across flooded creeks and billabongs? You must have a big four-wheel drive truck hidden away." His face was a picture. "And a truck driver?"

"Three hundred kilometres," she squawked. "What's that in miles?" She did the quick calculation in her head. "That can't be right. My directions said that Daly River is the closest town to Cockatoo Springs. That's why I drove down here from the airport."

"It is." He nodded sagely. "This is the outback."

Chapter Three

Alex almost felt sorry for the woman sitting across the table from him.

Almost.

He knew how hard food journalists from the top magazines had been trying to get an interview with his alter ego, managing director of Cockatoo Springs, Alessandro Ricardo, and it made hi angry . He'd only taken up the position at the request of his dead fiancée's family. They'd set the school up in her memory. He'd agreed and signed a two year contract on the strict condition he was a silent partner; it was a way he could get rid of the insurance payout from the accident. He didn't want the money, but he hadn't wanted to tarnish Emily's memory for her family. It was enough that he'd been hurt by what she'd done. Her family didn't need to know about it.

The promotional side of it drove him crazy. The stupid idea of him taking on an exotic sounding name as a figurehead for the school had been his assistant manager's idea. Mitch reckoned it was a way to keep away from the media, but it had backfired, and for some reason everyone wanted to know all about him. Christ, he was a lawyer and since he'd come to the Territory, he was happiest outdoors, messing about with his boats and crab traps once the school had been set up. He'd used his contacts to promote the place, and once they had Clay Bardi on board, a well-known indigenous chef who'd trained in London, chefs from all over the world had clamoured to get in.

The last thing Alex wanted to be was be some sort of celebrity figurehead and the subject of gossip magazines. But the media had latched onto the mysterious managing director of the Cockatoo Springs resort since they'd been named top restaurant in that blasted magazine, and the more he resisted, the harder they tried to get the scoop interview. Things had gotten out of hand, from helping a family out to being trapped by his fake identity. He just wanted it over.

Gutter press. He despised them. His life was private and it was staying that way.

One reporter had even infiltrated his kitchen in the guise of a kitchen hand. Another one had registered as a guest in the resort and tried to get an interview with him via his bed. Sultry-eyed Catalina from *Hot Food* magazine had been bundled out unceremoniously clutching her shoes and bag to her chest when he had thrown her out of his private suite. She'd got the sex…but not the interview. Now here was another one after an exclusive. He'd been enjoying the conversation with Jess until she'd dropped the bit about being there to interview him. Lying women and the media. Two things that peed him off most.

No way, baby. You are in for a rude shock. But this one interested him.

What's the Top End? And this is the closest tow*n,* he mimicked to himself. She was green.

He still wasn't sure if she was being totally honest with him. If she was with a magazine like she said, they would have at least organised her travel. He ran his hand along his chin and thought quickly. He was not going to get caught out again. He could send her back to Darwin and tell her to get the helicopter in, but the best way to ensure she didn't get a back door entry to Cockatoo Springs was to keep her close. And she needed to be taught a lesson in honesty. He was sick and tired of the subterfuge of so-called professionals trying to get an interview with Ricardo under false pretences.

He looked across the table through the flickering flame of the candle. The wax had run down the bottle and was gathering in white waxy splotches on Janet's red tablecloth. Jess was chewing on her bottom lip. An ache settled in his chest as a memory of Emily flitted through his mind.

But for the car accident, she would have had to tell him how she'd been about to dump him for a new man. Instead, he'd found out about it after the funeral when the guy had requested a meeting with him. So, he'd dealt with grief, and dealt with lies. He'd never told a soul but he'd vowed never to get sucked in by a woman again.

Now, this one was looking at him wide-eyes as he tried to warn her off.

"The freeway looked fairly civilised to me as I drove down this afternoon," she said. "I think you're just trying to scare me."

Alex shrugged and turned his concentration to his meal and his thoughts. Damn woman had bought the past back with a vengeance.

"The Top End is rough…and dangerous. It's no place for a woman travelling alone," he said gruffly.

Especially one clad in designer clothes and stiletto shoes. But he kept that thought to himself.

Emily had chewed her lip when she was upset. He quickly buried that thought. The only time he allowed himself to think of that time in his life—pre Cockatoo Springs days—was when his loud and boisterous family came up to stay. Only then did he dwell on the past and what could have been. He'd found out after the funeral that she'd been ready to leave him. So, he'd dealt with grief, and dealt with lies. He'd never told a soul, but he'd vowed never to get sucked in by a woman again.

The transformation of a grief stricken and

disillusioned lawyer into the barramundi fisherman and businessman he was now had been a long, hard road for him, and Alex guarded his privacy fiercely. Sex was for fun and pleasure. He kept his heart right out of it. There was no way he ever wanted to experience loss like he had when he'd lost Emily.

To death and deception.

If it hadn't been for the efforts of Nick and Tom, his two older brothers, he wondered if he would have ever picked up the pieces of his life. Now he intended to move on as soon as Clay, the new chef settled in. His contract was coming to an end in a few weeks. He'd achieved what he'd promised Emily's parents and more, and he wanted no publicity, no interviews, and magazine articles. He just wanted to fade into the background and let go of that stupid identity that seemed to fascinate everyone. Reality TV was responsible for most of this attitude. They thought they had an open door into anyone's life these days.

"Alex, are you listening to me?" Jess's voice intruded on his thoughts and he pushed his plate away.

"Sorry, what did you say?"

"I asked you which would be the best road to take to Cockatoo Springs tomorrow." Jess stared at him intently, and an unwelcome surge of desire hit him as he held her gaze. Her almond-shaped eyes were wide and her expression vulnerable as she worried at her bottom lip. A lush, full bottom lip.

Christ, she'd intended driving that little red box of a car across to the coast? He had to get the message across to her; if anything happened to her, he would feel bloody responsible.

"And I've told you already it is three hundred kilometres across flooded creeks and rough roads," he said.

Jess sat there with a frown wrinkling her brow. The bright red lipstick had disappeared between eating and choking fits, and he softened a little when despair clouded her face.

"Look, I'm sorry but there's no way you can drive in to Cockatoo Springs. The road from here is only for four-wheel drive vehicles. You'll have to drive back to Darwin and fly in."

A tear spilled onto her cheek, and she brushed it away impatiently. "Ignore me," she said brusquely. "I hardly ever cry. I'm just so disappointed and angry with myself." She plopped her elbows on the table and cradled her chin in her hands. "I'm always messing up. I do great work, but I'm not very good at organising myself." A rueful smile crossed her lips. "And this time, it means I've blown any chance of getting this interview…and my job.

Alex couldn't believe that any magazine would send a journalist this far without proper organisation and then sack them when they didn't deliver. If there was one thing he had kept from his law days, it was his sense of justice and fairness.

And integrity.

He hated lies and deception, and would be pleased when Alessandro Ricardo could disappear next month when the contract was up. Just because he kept to himself and didn't share his background with anyone, he still operated with honesty and integrity and truth… well, most of the time.

"Maybe I can help out." He was surprised when the words came from his mouth before his brain kicked in.

The look of hope that crossed her face tugged at his vulnerability. All three brothers were suckers for helpless females. Nick and Tom had both been lucky in life and love and were happily married and working on a tribe of kids to add to the Richards' clan. Tom and Brianna and their baby twins were in Italy, and Nick and Lissy lived in New Zealand with their toddler. Alex had no intention of going down the marriage path. It was not for him. Not now. Not ever.

"How are you going to help me?" she asked. "Find me a helicopter? I guess I'm going to have to drive back to Darwin and get myself organised."

He could arrange a helicopter for her with one phone call if he wanted, but after giving it some thought, he decided to offer her a lift out. *Keep the enemy close*. Once they got to Cockatoo Springs, he would decide how to handle her and he could always chopper her back to Darwin then. Whatever the outcome, there was no way she would ever find out who he was. And she needed a lesson in telling the truth.

He was Alex Richards, barramundi fisherman from the wild.

"I'm driving out there early tomorrow. If you trust me, I can give you a ride. Janet will vouch for me." He pointed to her meal. "Now enjoy your first foray into bush tucker before Janet brings out the spiced blood plum crumble I can smell cooking. I leave at five thirty in the morning."

***

After they'd eaten the dessert and finished with coffee, Alex stood and pushed his chair in. "If you decide to accept the lift be outside the office. On time."

Jess watched as he walked to the door. The tight jeans that hugged his butt outlined long muscular legs. She glanced back at Janet as she cleared the table.

"I can't believe the resort isn't close by." Jess shook her head.

"It's a decent enough drive in the dry," Janet said. "But with the wet starting early, the short road won't open up again till April. They've just opened a new bridge and that gives the tourists a better chance of getting up the river for the fishing."

"Thank you, and for the food. It was amazing."

The older woman's face lit up. "You think this is good, wait till you eat out at Cockatoo Springs." She put her head to the side. "You are going with him, aren't you? Alex Richards is a good man and I don't say that lightly. He's done it tough, but he's made a go of carting fish out of the river here for a couple of seasons. He's a gentleman and he'll get you to the resort in one piece."

Jess followed Janet across to the bar. "I'll settle my bill up now. Is there somewhere I can leave the rental car?"

"Leave the keys with me and I'll get my fella to put it in one of the sheds. How long are you going to stay out there?"

"Oh, not long. Just till I meet Alessandro Ricardo. I hope he's there." She sighed. "In my usual fashion I just tore over here. I didn't even think he might not be there. Anyway, if he's not there, I'll chase him down wherever he is."

Janet grinned. "Oh, don't worry, dear. He'll be there. I have no doubt about that."

###

It was still pitch dark when the alarm went off on Jess's phone the next morning. She ran the shower on cool water and tried to wake up—she was never at her best in the morning and certainly not before sunrise. She scrabbled through her suitcase looking for something suitable to wear in a fishing truck. Silky skirts, wraparound sarongs, and strappy sandals piled up on the bed as she searched for something more suitable. Finally, she came across a pair of white knee-length Capri pants and teamed them with a loose silk top that knotted at the waist. The sandals would just have to do because she had packed no substantial footwear.

She'd been expecting a resort, not a fishing outpost, a two-star caravan park, and a smelly truck. She glanced down at her watch as she searched for a pair of dangly earrings. She had to look the part when they arrived. After all, it was one of the luxury resorts in Australia.

As soon as they hit the road, she would have to ring or email and make a booking. There had been no phone service last night, and she couldn't check her email or call Monica to report in. Probably because of the storm.

Oh, shit. It was twenty-five minutes past the hour and she only had five minutes to get out the front to meet him. Forgetting the earrings, she flung everything back into her suitcase, slung her handbag over her shoulder, and with one swipe of her hand dropped her array of cosmetics into the small carryon bag. She grabbed her laptop and opened the door, and was blinded by the bright headlights of a truck driving up slowly from the back of the hotel.

It pulled up next to her, and by the smell of the fishing crates drifting from the back of the truck she knew her lift had arrived.

Alex opened his door and came around the front of the truck and looked at her bags.

"Sorry. They'll have to go in the back."

She held up her laptop and clutched it to her chest. "I'll hold this one."

"I have to pick up my dog and then we'll get going."

Jess looked at the back of the truck, loaded high with crates. He'd lifted the lid off a huge one and stowed her luggage into it. She'd never get the fish smell out of it.

"Where does the dog sit? In the back?"

"Up front," he said with a smile. "You're taking his seat. You'll have to nurse him."

Before she could reply, he flashed her a grin and walked around to the other side of the truck and swung himself up. She bit back a rude retort and heaved her laptop onto her other shoulder as he leaned across the cabin and opened the door for her.

She hated dogs. Ever since one of those little white fluffy toy things her mother always carted around bit her.

"Jump in."

She climbed into the truck and put her laptop and bag down where she could find a space amongst the assortment of nets and small, coloured, plastic fish covering the floor. Alex turned the truck out onto the main road. The dawn sky was a soft rosy apricot to the east. They travelled a few kilometres in silence before he took a turn across a high bridge and then onto a narrow dirt road that led down to the river. He pulled up outside a small shed surrounded by fishing nets and more of the huge blue crates that she was getting used to.

"No need for you to get out. I'll just unload the crates and pick up Bowser, hook up the boat, and then we'll be on the way." He looked at her steadily in the dimly lit cabin and his expression dared her not to comment on his dog's name.

"The boat? We have to take a boat to get there?" Jess tried to keep her voice calm, but it came out as an undignified squawk.

Alex climbed out of the truck and turned to her before he shut the door.

"No, I need the boat to check my crab traps in the rivers on the way to Cockatoo Springs." Jess let out a breath and sat for a few minutes wondering what the day ahead was going to bring. Once boredom set in, she pulled her phone out, pleased to see the service bars were strong again. Once her email downloaded, she checked messages and sent off a quick text to Mon.

Almost there. Will call when we arrive. Then she deleted *we* and replaced it with *I* before she pressed send. Her phone buzzed almost instantly as the reply came in.

Are u staying out of trouble?

No way was she going to tell Monica what she was doing. She would hear the screech across the ocean.

Always. Call you tonight. Ciao.

She leaned back, yawned, and closed her eyes. The crashing and banging from the back of the truck overlaid the muffled conversation and the occasional laughter drifting though her window.

She would kill for a coffee.

A few minutes later, her wish was fulfilled when the aroma of coffee drifted through the cabin of the truck. She rubbed her eyes with the heels of her hands and reached out for the huge travel mug Alex passed through the open window.

"White, no sugar. Same as last night," he said passing her a coffee and a brown paper bag. "Muffins, not bush tucker, I'm afraid, but just as good. My mate, Wally's missus just made a batch and they're still warm. I called her last night and she's packed our tucker for the trip."

"I must have drifted off," Jess said sleepily. "Thank you." She sat up and peeked into the paper bag and the aroma made her mouth water even more. "Tucker? Do you mean bush tucker?"

"No. Tucker is food."

"This will do me till we get there," she said. "I'm still getting over that glorious meal last night."

"I doubt it will last you that long" Alex shook his head. "We'll probably get there late tomorrow, but if we strike any problems, we may have to camp out for two nights."

"What?" Jess's stomach plummeted and she stiffened in the seat. "Camp out? What do you mean camp out?"

"Do you ever listen?" Alex asked patiently. "I said last night the river is up and we're probably going to have to go the long way."

He opened the truck door and whistled. A quick scratching noise was the only warning Jess got before a brindle staffy jumped onto the seat and pushed his nose into her lap.

"Jess, meet Bowser." With a soft groan, she held her coffee high out of the dog's reach it as he sniffed around her arms and legs.

Oh, damn, I've really messed up this time.

Chapter Four

Finishing the last of her coffee, Jess placed the empty travel cup next to Alex's in the square console between the two seats. The dawn sky was light by the time Alex had jumped back into the pickup and swung it out on the main road. She turned around and peered through the back window to see what was rattling behind them, but a sheet of khaki-coloured canvas blocked her view. Moving closer to the window, she stared outside at the flat, boring landscape as the sun cleared the horizon, ignoring the little dog whose serious gaze was fixed unblinkingly on her face.

Not one word had passed between them since Alex placed the dog on her lap. Morning had broken and the sun began its climb into the vast outback sky. The landscape was monotonous and there was nothing to look at apart from high tussock grass and termite mounds that edged the road. The red dusty road stretched ahead in a straight line as far as she could see. In the far distance, plumes of white and dark brown smoke rose in the brilliant blue sky, and she glanced across at Alex who was intent on the road ahead. His long hair hung untidily over his collar and he'd rolled up his sleeves a few miles back. His tanned forearms arms were bare, and his right elbow rested casually on the open window frame.

"That's not a bushfire ahead, is it?" She pointed to the south…no… it would be the north; she was in a different hemisphere now and her sense of direction had gone completely AWOL.

"Ah, she speaks." The amused tone in his voice fired up Jess's temper, and she bit down the smart retort that sprang to her lips. After all, he was doing her a favour and it was his truck.

"I was drinking my coffee. It was very nice." She injected a sweetness into her voice she was not feeling. "Thank you."

"No, don't stress, it's not a bushfire. The savannah woodlands are burned off in the dry season every year," he said. "We're just coming into the wet now, so that should be the last of the fires once the rains come and stay."

She nodded and turned back to stare out the window, fighting the queasy feeling in her stomach. The truck bounced over the corrugations in the unpaved road, and the noise of the motor roared through the open window on his side of the truck. Diesel fumes wafted in, occasionally overlaid by the smell of fish.

"Are you travelling okay?" Alex asked as the truck hit a dip in the road and bounced hard.

She could have sworn he was getting

amusement from her situation. His voice was full of mirth, but when she glanced across at him, his expression was serious and he was looking at the road ahead. Looking down, she tried to relax her hands, which were in a death grip in her lap, and straightened her legs out in the confined space on the floor.

"Yes, I'm fine, thank you," she said.

Hours and hours to go. She was blocking the thought of the journey ahead from her mind and focusing on each moment, and there were a lot of moments ahead if this was going to take a day, or God forbid more. *Plan the article in your head, store the description of the landscape, and think about the luxurious resort waiting for you at the end.*

Two days to go. How the hell did she get herself in this situation?

And a night camping in the outback? Maybe two?

There was no way she was going to tell anyone how badly she'd messed things up this time. No one besides the fisherman and Janet from the caravan park would ever know how irresponsible she'd been. Last time she'd forgotten to book a room, she'd been in Sri Lanka with Mon and her boyfriend, Gareth, and they'd shared their hotel room with her. She grinned to herself. It sure had cramped their style having her on the sofa in their luxurious bedroom.

I can do it.

Why in hell did she decide to drive to this place? If she'd known there was a helicopter out there from Darwin, she would have caught that, and would be by now sitting around a pool, soaking up the sun and planning how to get her interview. It probably left from the same airport she'd flown into. And then there was the problem of getting back to Daly River to sort out the rental car. As soon as she was settled at Cockatoo Springs, she'd ring the rental company and arrange for a pick up. It might cost a fortune, but it would be less bother than trying to get back to Daly River to collect it. Next time, she'd listen to Monica and get herself organised.

The truck hit another rut in the road and her laptop case pressed into her legs. It was jammed between the backs of her knees and the floor, and she leaned forward to push it to the side.

"Put it behind the seat to give yourself some more leg room." The laconic drawl was followed quickly by a curse. "Oh shit, hang on."

A loud bang echoed through the truck just as Jess leaned down to reach for the laptop. The truck bounced hard and slewed to the right as Alex swung the wheel hard and hit the brakes at the same time. Her head banged against the window, and when the vehicle bounced over the rocks on the side of the road, the top of her head hit the back of the seat so hard it jarred her neck. Without thinking, she grabbed for the little dog that had landed on the floor at her feet, and held him tightly on her lap. The truck came to an abrupt halt. Red dust rose in a cloud around the cabin, and she waved her hand and coughed.

"Sorry about that. That hole was filled with bull dust, and I didn't see it coming." Alex opened his door and looked across at her with a frown. "Is your head okay? You hit the seat with a fair thump."

"I'm fine, thank you. It's the dust that's the worst."

Alex reached into the side of the door and passed her a bottle of water.

"Hang on to Bowser, will you? I don't want him taking off here."

"What are you doing?" The dog began to whimper when Alex got out of the car and tried to make a break for it. She held on to him tightly, terrified he would turn around and bite her. She so didn't do dogs.

"I'm going to check the truck. I want to make sure we didn't do any damage to the wheel when we hit that hole." He slammed the door and Jess put her head back and closed her eyes as the dog's whimpering turned into a full-blown howl. The truck swayed from side to side, and a few bangs and crashes spurred the dog onto even louder howls.

"Bowser, shut up!" The dog stopped howling and took up the high-pitched whimper again. At the same time, a stench wafted from his nether regions. Jess shoved the dog away and held it at arm's length, turning her head toward the window as the truck began to sway. She opened her eyes and craned forward as it rocked from side to side. Alex was gripping the big bar at the front of the pickup and as Jess watched he pushed at it again until the car rocked even harder. His T-shirt moulded to his chest and his muscles flexed as he strained against the weight of the car.

"Can I help?" she called out. For some reason her breath caught in her throat. It was the dust, not the eye candy at the front of the car causing the flutter in her chest.

"Nah, it's fine, thanks." With one final push, the car stopped rocking and he stepped back and looked down with a grin. "No major damage."

Alex reached in through the window across Jess. As he retrieved a dog leash from behind her seat, his forearm brushed across her breasts, and she jumped as a tingle shot through to her nipples. He called the dog over to the window. "Come on, little fella. Wee break." He clipped the leash onto the Bowser's collar and lifted the small dog through the open window.

"Do you need one yet?"

"One what?"

"A washroom break. Been a while since you finished that coffee."

"No, thank you," she said primly. "I'll wait for the next roadhouse."

Alex put his head back and laughed. The blasted dog joined in and barked until she put her hands over her ears.

His long-sleeved button-through shirt was open at the neck and the corded muscles of his tanned throat stood out as he clutched the dog to his chest. He stopped laughing and grinned at her.

"Sorry, sweetheart. None of them on this road."

"None of what?"

"Roadhouses."

"Well, how long till we get back to a main highway?" Jess folded her arms as uncertainty curled through her chest.

"This *is* the main road. We turn off onto the back road in about another hundred kilometres."

The sick feeling was firmly back in her stomach, and this time it had nothing to do with the odours in the truck.

***

Alex tried to keep the grin off his face. Teaching little Miss America a lesson in honesty was going to be so much easier than he'd thought. And she'd almost jumped a mile when he'd accidentally brushed against her before. He'd been peeved with himself when the blood kicked to his groin as her nipples had peaked through the silk shirt. Why not? A bit of fun wouldn't hurt?

He shook his head and put Bowser onto the ground, pointing to the other side of the vehicle.

"If you change your mind, there's a grove of melaleucas over there, just through the spear grass. The trees with the papery bark. And there's a roll of toilet tissue in the glove compartment."

She shook her head and leaned back on the seat, closing her eyes.

"Watch out for snakes, if you do change your mind."

He walked to the back of the truck and checked the boat was secure on the trailer before he headed off into the long grass with Bowser. He picked his way carefully through the cracked and dry ground between the termite mounds across to a clump of boulders. To his surprise, the ground was dry. The way the Daly River had come up last night he'd thought the rain had been more widespread. They'd only travelled forty kilometres to the west and it appeared there'd been no rain here at all. The weather was in their favour if that was the case. If the road stayed this dry all the way to Peppinmenarti, he'd be able to double back on the Port Keats road and save them some time. It all depended on how long the rains stayed away.

After waiting for the dog to lift his leg on every boulder in sight, Alex headed back to the truck.

Jess was leaning forward and looking into the distance.

"It's a long way, and the road's corrugated, but if it stays dry, we'll take the short cut." Alex opened the door and lifted Bowser into the truck. The dog scurried across the seat and jumped straight onto Jess's lap, trailing red dusty footprints across her pants. She scowled.

Miss America was in a fine mood this morning.

"There's a packet of dog snacks in the glove compartment." When Jess didn't move, Alex reached across in front of her, deliberately brushing his arm against her bare knees before he opened the compartment. Bowser's ears pricked up as the packet of liver treats rustled. A dollop of slobber hung from his jaw as he sniffed the air.

"Ew." Jess pushed him off her lap, but she wasn't quick enough. The slobber dropped onto her forearm and she wiped it on her white shorts.

"Oh, how disgusting." She crossed her arms and the silk strained across her generous breasts.

Alex laughed. "Sorry, he does have some bad habits. He's old enough to know better, but he's never learned."

The look she gave him showed she had begun to place him on a similar social scale as the dog. He was getting under her skin already and he hadn't even tried.

Good.

Jess didn't reply as she scrubbed her arm, smearing a wet patch onto the fabric of her pants. Finally, she heaved a big breath and turned to him.

"So how long will that take? Will we get there today if we go the short way?" She pushed the dog away and brushed at the marks on her legs.

"No, we'll still have one night under the stars."

She pursed her lips. "There's no need to make it sound like a holiday. I'll do that when we get to the resort. So, tell me about it. Why is it so far from everywhere?"

Alex looked across at her considering how much to tell her. He could tell her a little about the resort and she could do her article, if that was what she was really here for. But no interview with him. She wouldn't ever know who he was. When they stopped for lunch, he'd call Mitch on the satellite phone and see whether the first of the rains had hit Cockatoo Springs last night, and prime him about keeping the Alessandro Ricardo bit quiet when they arrived. One night should be enough to teach Miss America her lesson about survival in the outback and deceiving people to get what she wanted.

"It's on the edge of what they call the Kimberley region, one of the last remaining remote areas in Australia. It's a base for seeing lakes, diamond mines, and exploring the indigenous culture. The bush tucker school started up a couple of years ago."

"I heard they've snaffled one of the top London chefs to run the school."

"Yes, Clay Bardi is an indigenous guy who was raised in the Kimberley region, and he trained as a chef in Darwin before moving to Europe and taking the restaurant world by storm." He grinned at her. "Alessandro pulled a real coup getting him for the school."

"So, tell me about Alessandro. Is he as elusive as they say? And why when he's built up such a great school. Is he a chef, too or just the owner?"

"Look." Alex leaned across and pointed out her window. "Emus." He started the truck and diesel fumes entered through his window in a puff of black smoke.

"You might be used to this." She waved her arm and pointed a red manicured finger to the large birds running across the bare red dirt. "But it's a very different experience for me."

"Hmm, your trip from Broadway to LA wasn't quite as rough as this?"

"Oh, for goodness sake, I told you my real

story last night. And I don't usually drive anywhere, I fly." Jess gagged and waved her hand in the air to clear the smoke. "Can you please close your window and put the air conditioning on? That smells disgusting."

Alex gunned the motor and the truck bounced sharply as it lurched over the rocks on the side of the road. Bowser finished chewing his snack and jumped back onto Jess's lap as the speed of the truck picked up.

"Sorry, love. Air con already on. It's a two by eighty system."

She turned to him with a frown. Beads of perspiration dotted her top lip, and she reached down the front of her top and pulled out a tissue, gently dabbing her face. His gaze lingered on the soft swell of her generous breasts beneath her shirt, and his blood heated as he took in the view.

"What's that?"

"Eighty kilometres per hour, two windows down." He lifted his gaze from the soft shadow between her breasts and nodded to her window. "If you're hot, wind it down. She's an old truck, and the air con died a couple of years back."

He reached over and grabbed his dog from her lap. "I'll hang on to him, though. He likes to stick his head out in the breeze." Jess leaned forward and grunted as she wound the window lever until the window stuck halfway down.

"Sorry, that's as far as it goes," he said. "Keep meaning to fix it, but I've been too busy with the fish and the crabs."

Bowser settled onto the seat between them and curled up to sleep. The road smoothed out and no more unexpected potholes appeared in front of the truck. They were getting close to the turn off to the shortcut. He glanced across at Jess as she pulled her phone from her pocket and stared at the screen.

"No point looking at that here. You might as well turn it off and save your battery. There's no mobile service all the way from here to the coast."

She shoved it into her bag on the floor. Her face lit up when she smiled up at him. She really was a looker. Shame she was less than honest.

"I'm not used to being disconnected. Might not be a bad thing. I spend too much time on social media these days."

Alex gestured down to her feet. "You've never been to the outback before?"

She shook her head. "I've never been to Australia before."

"I'll lend you a pair of socks when we stop. Those shoes aren't strong enough for out here. Be careful when you get out of the truck. The grass seeds of the black spear grass are very sharp, and if you step on one, it will go straight through those flimsy shoes." He looked at her, trying to figure out if she was as scatterbrained as her planning made her seem. "So, tell me about Jess Trent…really a former or wannabe actress, or always a journalist?"

"I'm just a wannabe journo out looking for a good story."

"Long way to come looking."

He glanced over when she didn't reply, and she looked away.

Definitely hiding something or not being quite truthful. Not what he needed or wanted.

The truck skittered across the potholes between the long ruts that had formed from the runoff from the heavy rains last wet season. The only sound for the next half hour was Bowser's snoring on the seat between them. Alex focused all his attention on the road. The corrugations were getting worse the further west they travelled.

"Ah, Alex."

"Yes? What's up?" He turned his attention to her for a moment. He hadn't noticed Bowser crawl back over to Jess. The small dog was curled up on her lap and her fingers were loosely threaded through his collar.

"Could we have that washroom stop soon?" Jess was looking at the window and her brow was wrinkled. "There are no trees?"

"Yup. You're right. There's no trees."

"So, what do I do?"

"I guess it depends how much you need a stop."

They'd been travelling for a while so he guessed it was as good a time as any to take another break. He pulled the truck to the side of the road, and the red dust billowed in through the passenger window. Jess waved her hand in front of her face as she coughed, and Bowser jumped off her lap.

Alex looped the leash through the dog's collar, and climbed out waiting for Bowser to follow him, but he turned in a circle and settled back on the seat. Jess stayed in her seat as well until he walked around and opened her door.

"I thought you needed a stop."

"I do." She swung her legs through the door and looked down at the bare dirt at the side of the road before lifting her gaze to meet his. "Are there any snakes here?"

"Sweetheart, there is nothing here." He spread his arms wide and followed her gaze as she leaned out and looked around. Deep blue sky, big sky, contrasted with the bare red dirt. The only thing breaking the flat, red vista was the narrow road heading west in a perfectly straight, unbroken line.

"No self-respecting creature would survive out here." Alex took pity on her as she looked hesitantly at the rough ground. She let out a soft gasp when he reached in and lifted her out, letting her slide down the front of him to the ground. A prickle of awareness shot through him as her soft breasts pressed against his chest, and he held her longer than necessary.

"I'll get back in the truck with Bowser, and close my eyes while you go around the back of the truck and use the…er…washroom." He shrugged. "Sorry, we don't have five-star facilities in the outback.

"Looks to me like you don't have any facilities." She stepped gingerly toward the back of the truck and waited for him to get back in.

Alex hoisted himself up into this seat. He lifted Bowser onto his lap and waited. "What do you reckon, little buddy? She's a looker, isn't she?" All he got was a snuffle in reply.

He leaned his head back on the seat and closed his eyes while he waited.

"Alex!" The shrill scream turned his blood to ice.

Chapter Five

Jess stood in the boat on the trailer behind the truck, her eyes fixed on the two strange looking creatures running across the dirt toward the road. Luckily, she'd been adjusting her clothing when she'd heard the sound, and without thinking she'd jumped up into the boat behind the truck.

Alex's laugh reached her as he appeared around the side.

"Jeez, don't panic. They won't come near us."

"What are they?" She kept her gaze fixed on the back of the creatures as their ungainly gait took them away from the road.

"Emus. I pointed them out to you before."

"They look different close up."

Alex held out his hand and Jess stepped up on the side of the boat. When she moved, her shoe caught in the coil of rope beneath her feet and she pitched headfirst over the side. Before she knew it, two strong arms were around her, and her face was buried in Alex's neck. Her heart was thudding and beat faster when she looked up and saw tanned skin almost against her lips. Strong corded muscles stood out in his neck, and a woodsy masculine smell she hadn't noticed before assailed her senses. She closed her eyes as embarrassment filled her, pushing away the temptation to slide her lips over that smooth skin.

"Sorry, I tripped." She pushed her arms against his chest, but he still held her tightly.

"Put me down, please. Can we just get back on the road and get as far as we can today?"

Alex carried her around the side of the truck and put her down before he opened the door. "You don't want a coffee break?" he said with a grin.

She looked around at the barren landscape surrounding them. The sooner they got going, the sooner she could get back to civilisation. And away from this guy who was unsettling her.

"No, just drive."

###

Jess leaned back into the seat and took a deep breath.

"Why don't you try and catch a nap?" Alex reached beneath the seat and threw her a small bottle of water.

"Thanks." She took a swig of the now warm water and recapped the bottle, and put it on the floor near her feet. Leaning her head back, she closed her eyes and tried to doze off, but the constant jarring of the hard road made it impossible, and Jess began to worry about the situation she'd got herself into.

Never again. When I get back to New York, I'll plan everything I do. No more rushing into situations without thinking them through first.

She'd messed up every part of her life over the past few years and now as a last resort she'd put all her effort getting this job to try and turn things around. She didn't need to work but she'd cut ties with her family. After the fiasco with Harrison, her ex-fiancé, she'd realised talking about her famous father and his wealth only brought trouble to her life. After she'd broken off the engagement she'd changed her surname from Van Lund to Trent, her mother's maiden name.

Overhearing Harrison's conversation with his best man at the rehearsal dinner the night before the wedding had opened her eyes. Not only was he after the money and prestige of joining the Van Lund family business by marrying her, he still had his girlfriend on the side. And his smarmy, preppy best man had the gall to congratulate him on his double accomplishment not realising Jess was standing right behind him. The look on Harrison's face had been priceless, and had told her all she needed to know.

The purpose of the rehearsal dinner had been for the relatives and friends of the bride and groom to meet and have a good time. Well, they'd met and no one had a good time, because Jess had fronted Harrison in front of everyone, outed the girlfriend, and left town that night. She chuckled to herself. At least she could see the funny side of it now.

"Can't sleep?" Alex's deep voice interrupted her thoughts, and she grinned.

"Yes, I was just thinking about something funny that happened to me before I moved to New York."

And it had been funny. She realised she'd been pushed into the whole thing because all he'd been after was her family connection, and her father after had been in cahoots with them. She'd had no regrets, shed no tears, and it had been a lucky escape. But since she'd started work with Larry's company, she'd not touched a penny of her trust fund. Her father had said she would come crawling back to him for money, and she'd decided she would live on the street before she ever touched another cent of the family fortune again. If he could treat her like that, their relationship was toast.

"Tell me about life in the Big Apple." Alex glanced across at her.

"Okay. So, you want to know a little bit about me?" She turned in the seat and tucked her legs beneath her, facing him. He turned his attention back to the road, but with one arm resting on the window and the other lightly holding the steering wheel as the truck moved smoothly down the straight road.

"I live in New York and until recently I shared an apartment with my best friend, Monica. I work for a media company and I hate my job. I found out recently I only got it because my father pulled strings with one of his buddies." She bit off her words, she'd said more than she'd intended to. "Anyway, a great job has come up, and if I get this interview with Alessandro Ricardo it will give me a great chance of getting it."

"You want this job so bad you'll travel to the outback without booking a hotel, on the off chance of getting an interview with someone who doesn't give interviews?" He shook his head as he looked across at her curiously.

"Yes, I'll do anything to get it." She turned to him. "If you knew me better, you'd know I am determined. I'll try as hard as I can to pull this one off."

"Really?"

"I only have one shot at this. There is a full-time position open, and I know at least three journalists who are going after it."

"A city job? Or out in the field?" He turned his head briefly from the road and looked at her. "I'd hate being in an office. Give me my boat and a good catch of fish any day."

"You're lucky if you're happy that way, and you can run your business like that. I'm already having withdrawals because I can't check my phone out here."

"So, what will you do if you don't get this interview?"

"Oh, I'll get it. I have to. If I don't, it means I have to sell my apartment because I won't stay in the job I've got now."

He looked back to the road and she glanced up at him. A slight smile curled his lips and the crinkles deepened around his eyes. "I'm impressed with your determination. So, what are you going to do? Turn up and knock on Ricardo's door and demand an interview? You've got some balls."

"No." She laughed. This guy had no idea how the world of cutthroat business worked. She'd been brought up in the thick of it and knew all the tricks but she'd never lowered herself to that level before now. Maybe meeting Alex had been fortuitous. "You said you worked out of Cockatoo Springs?"

"Yup, I do."

"So." Jess grasped her hands together in front of her chest and stared at him. "Do you know him? Have you ever met Ricardo?"

Alex grinned at her, lifted his hand from the window, and gestured down to his work clothes.

"Who me? A simple fisherman?"

Disappointment surged through her. That would have been the easiest way to get an introduction if Alex knew Ricardo.

"Have you made an appointment for the interview?" he asked.

"No, not exactly."

"Not exactly?" He flicked her a glance. "No hotel room booked, and no appointment? You like to live on the edge."

"He doesn't do interviews so that's why I can't book it, smarty-pants. I called from New York. I couldn't get past his secretary."

"Tell me, what are you doing here all the way from New York if he doesn't do interviews?"

"I am going to do my best to get one… somehow."

"An expensive trip for an interview you don't even have lined up."

"I'm in Australia, I'm on my way to the resort now, and the next step will be to get the interview." Jess dropped her hands to her lap and looked down. "This has turned out okay so far."

Alex threw his head back and laughed. "Turned out okay? That's how you ended up in my old truck heading across the outback with shoes and clothes fit for a night out? Oh yeah, you did that very well."

"Don't be rude, that sunrise was just one tiny, little mistake."

"You're telling me you've done worse?"

Jess tipped her head back on the headrest and cursed as her loose hair snagged on the chipped leather. She leaned forward and reached down into her bag for a clip.

"Oh yeah, a lot worse. But I got the interview." She turned and grinned at him as she held her up above her head with one hand.

"Tell me about it."

Jess gave up looking for a clip and her hair dropped down around her neck again. She leaned forward so it wouldn't snag on the headrest.

"Maybe later."

"There's some string in the glove compartment. You'll be cooler with your hair tied up." He reached over, dropped the door opened, and passed her a ball of blue twine.

"You've got a whole grocery store in there."

"It's the boy scout in me. Be prepared, I always say." He snapped the door shut and turned his gaze back to the road. "I use it to tie the crab traps together when I'm travelling."

Jess tried to break off a length of string with her fingers, but it was too strong. Alex stretched back in the seat and dug in the pocket of his jeans with his left hand.

"I've got a knife in here, but I can't reach it." He gripped the steering wheel and stretched further back. "See if you can get it."

Heat ran up Jess's neck. The last thing she wanted to do was poke about in his jeans pocket.

She glanced over at him, and discomfort filled her as a small smile played about his lips. If that was how he wanted to get his thrills, no way was she going to play along. She sat up straight in the seat.

"It's okay. I'll wait till we stop." Opening the glove compartment, she shoved the ball of twine back in and a small box fell to the floor. She picked it up and pushed it back in and slammed the compartment shut. The heat from her neck ran up to her face and she was sure her skin was flaming red. She glanced over but his attention was on the road. A frisson of nerves jittered in her stomach as he turned and looked at her.

Talk about Mr. Be Prepared Boy Scout. How many fishermen carried a box of condoms in their fishing trucks?

Her expression must have been easy to read.

"Like I said, Jess. Be prepared. You never know your luck in the big city or so they say."

"Well, you're in the outback now, and you're out of luck." She stared out the window as he roared with laughter.

***

Alex glanced across at Jess. The heat and the discomfort of the trip were starting to get to her. Her face was bright red and perspiration trickled down the side of her neck. He glanced at his watch and did a quick calculation of the mileage on the odometer on the control panel.

"Only about half hour to go before we hit the turn off. We'll take a break just after that. There's a nice little clearing on the river not far off the road. No red dirt and no emus there."

The look on Jess's face was priceless. By the end of this trip, she'd be able to write an article about keeping safe in the outback.

She had her head back on the headrest and her eyes were closed. His gaze travelled up the long line of her throat up to the unblemished skin of her face. Her softly parted lips were full and tempting. He still had to decide how far he'd go in teaching her a lesson in honesty, but it certainly wasn't going to be an unpleasant experience.

All was quiet as they covered the last twenty kilometres to the turnoff, the silence punctuated only by Bowser's soft snuffling as he slept. Thunderheads built to the north, and Alex slowed the truck as he peered out the window. There was only a little while to go until he had to make the decision of either taking the short cut across to the coast or going around the long way through the tiny settlement of Peppinmenarti.

Damn. His permit to travel through the private Aboriginal land was back in the office at Cockatoo. He hadn't given it a thought when he'd headed off last week. That pretty much made the decision for him. Without a permit to enter Aboriginal land, they'd *have* to take the short track and he'd have to hope the rain held off for one more night. The turnoff to the northeast appeared on the right, and he swung the wheel hard as the tyres spun in the fine red bull dust. Bowser barked, and Jess opened her eyes and blinked.

"Are we there?" She stretched her arms above her head and cursed as her hair snagged on the rough headrest again. Leaning back onto it, she untangled her hair and held it up in a knot on the top of her head.

Alex grinned as Bowser clambered back over to her lap. "Sorry, the old girl's a bit shabby. Not a lot of money in fishing."

"I'll pay you for driving me over, of course," she said.

"No need, I was coming this way anyway. And you've already spent enough, I'd say, if you're not going to have a job."

"We'll see." Jess pointed out the windscreen ahead. "It's a lot greener up this way?"

"Yeah, we're close to the Daly River again. It winds its way to the coast in loops."

She wiped the perspiration of her brow with the back of her free hand and held her hair above her head. "Anywhere to swim when we stop?"

He looked at her with a frown. "If you've got a death wish."

"What?"

"Crocs."

"Here?"

"Yes, here. You really didn't do your research, did you?"

"I thought only the saltwater crocodiles were dangerous. Aren't we a long way from the salt water?"

"Yes, we are. But they're here too, plus the freshwaters will attack if you provoke them, too."

Jess looked across at him and her green eyes were wide. "You're teasing me, right?"

He shook his head. "When I offered to bring you across to Cockatoo Springs, the main reason I offered, was to keep you safe."

Well, that was *one* of the reasons he'd offered. And she certainly had shown him she had no idea about keeping herself safe.

"The saltwater crocodile is a man-eater and they've invaded the river and creek systems of the Top End. They come as far as three hundred kilometres inland, and here we're only about a hundred kilometres from the coast. We wind in and out across the wetlands to get back up to Cockatoo Springs. As the crow flies, it's only about a third of the distance we spend on the road."

"You're just trying to frighten me."

A lazy swirl of desire kicked low in his groin. *Not now. Not yet.*

"Look, Jess, I might have teased you about other things, but this is deadly serious and you have to listen to everything I say and do it when I say to. Okay?"

"Oh…okay, as long as you promise you are being truthful with me. No sharing a tent because you say you have to protect me or stuff like that, okay?"

Alex laughed. He hadn't thought of that one. It would have been good ploy to upset her. In fact, he hadn't given much thought to the camping at the waterfall…yet.

"Not a problem. We'll stay well back from the water, and besides, I don't have a tent."

"What, we sleep out in the open? No way."

"No, I'll sleep in my swag in the boat and you and Bowser can have the back of the truck."

"What? With all that the smelly fish stuff?"

"I unloaded that when we stopped at Wally's and put the canvas canopy on the back of the truck. It might still smell a bit, but it'll keep the mozzies off you."

"The what?"

"The mosquitoes. Don't you have them in the States?"

"Of course we do, it was your accent that threw me."

"Anyway, make sure you cover up with Bushman's. There's some in—"

"The glove compartment," she finished off his sentence with a laugh.

At least she had a sense of humour.

He idled the truck to a stop about seventy-five meters from the water beneath a stand of melaleuca trees, their ghostly white bark bright in the mid-morning sunshine. The water was low and flowing slowly where a narrow U-shaped bay came off the main arm of the river. Fringed by white sand and overhanging trees, it was one of his favourite stops on the road to his resort. It would have been a good stop for the night, but he wanted to cover more of the road before he called it quits for the day in case it began to rain.

Reaching behind the seat, he passed a long-sleeved khaki shirt to Jess.

"Put that on, it will protect you from the sun and the insects."

While he kept digging behind the seat for a pair of socks, Jess took it off him and wrinkled her nose.

"Sorry, it's a spare fishing shirt," he said. "Pretty hard to get away from the smell of fish when you're around my truck." After a minute, he held up a pair of black work socks and grinned at her. "Success. Put these on under your sandals." He opened his door and pointed to Bowser. "Stay there, boy."

The dog stopped, and ran back across the seat to Jess.

"No way. I'm not putting your socks on."

She threw them back over the seat and opened the door.

"Whatever, but don't come crying to get me to take the prickles out of your feet."

Walking around to the other side of the truck, he reached up to help her to climb down. She waved his hand away and jumped down onto the river sand, and stood there buttoning up the shirt while he cut a piece of string and passed it to her. She looked at it for a moment before she shrugged and tipped her head forward, gathering her hair in one hand and looping the string around it before tying it off.

"We'll stay here about half an hour. I've got some crab traps in the river I can check now, seeing we've come this way. Then we'll have a cuppa." He pointed to the stand of trees on the right. "There's a nice natural restroom over there. Just watch out for brown snakes."

"What about the crocodiles when you check the traps?"

"That's okay. When you come back from the 'restroom', I'll back the trailer down and drop the boat off. Do you want to come out in the boat and help me?"

"God, no. I'll wait in the truck."

Alex shrugged. "Offer's there if you change your mind."

***

Five minutes later, Jess stood and grinned as she adjusted her clothes. She tiptoed over to the area shield by the thick trees, and managed to avoid prickles and snakes. It was possible Alex might be exaggerating the dangers and trying to scare her. This restroom experience, out in the open under the trees, would be a story to tell in the office when she got home. For a New Yorker used to her creature comforts, she'd already learned a lot of new things in her experiences during the last twenty-four hours. Now that they were into the journey, her confidence had kicked back, despite being in the middle of nowhere with a total stranger with no company except for crocodiles, brown snakes, and mosquitoes.

And birds.

She looked up in appreciation as a flock of something black with bright red slashes in their tail feathers squawked overhead and settled in the trees above her.

"Red-Tailed Black Cockatoos." Alex sauntered over with Bowser on his leash trotting along beside him.

"They're beautiful."

"They're a protected species. Over at Cockatoo Springs, we—" He bit off his words and Jess looked at him.

"You what?

"Doesn't matter." He turned on his heel and

dragged Bowser behind him. "Come on, I have to get this boat in the water, so we can't stand around yakking all day."

She shrugged and followed, watching where she placed her almost-bare feet. Her sandals were pretty but flimsy, and offered little protection against any of the hazards he'd described. She'd be spending as much time as she could in the truck, and she was not going to put on those socks. Wrinkling her nose, she looked down. The smelly shirt was bad enough.

Alex paused at the boat trailer and lifted three big wire mesh circles out of the boat and put them on the ground. Jess kept walking and stopped behind the truck. The tray on the back was covered with a square tent-like abode made of thick khaki canvas. It was zipped up tight all round and two large canvas flaps were held down with plastic pegs.

He glanced up at her. "That's your room. Unzip it and check it out if you want." His tanned face broke into a grin. "I've already had your bags delivered."

Jess reached up, and unzipped the zipper on one side, but she couldn't reach the top. It was too high. She climbed up onto the draw bar of the trailer, unzipped it to the top, and peered into the dim space. A foam mattress with chunky holes eaten out of it, by something she had no desire to know of, filled the small space. Her bags were thrown in a jumble at one end, and an old discoloured pillow and a dirty blanket lay in a heap on the middle of the mattress.

"Sorry it's not five-star accommodation."

Jess jumped when Alex's breath grazed over her ear. It was immediately followed by his warm body pressing up against her back. He leaned forward and pointed into the little space. Jess stiffened as he moved closer, and he casually looped one arm across her shoulders.

"Bowser chewed up some of the mattress last time he slept in there, and it might not be pretty, but it's still comfy." He stepped down from the draw bar of the trailer and held his hand out to her. She gripped it and hitched her breath. A jolt of heat ran up her arm. As her feet hit the ground, she dropped his hand and stepped away.

"What do you want me to do?"

"Stay in the truck with Bowser while I've got the boat in the water. It won't take me long to lift the crab traps. With a bit of luck, you might even get crab for dinner." He grinned at her. "Won't be as good as Janet's fish, but you can still take a photo if you like."

He moved in closer and looked down at her. "Crab on a campfire by a waterfall. Would that give you a good article and help you keep your job?"

"It would help but it's not quite up there

with an interview with the famous Alessandro Ricardo and his chefs."

She moved back, feeling uncomfortable with his proximity. Alex was giving out mixed signals. Something wasn't right. He walked to the front of the truck and lifted Bowser back in before turning to her. "Can you back a trailer?"

"Can I what?"

"Just what I said. Drive the truck backward so the trailer goes straight in the water."

"Er...I don't know." And she certainly didn't want to try it.

"What say we give it a go? A lot safer for me if I can stay in the boat while you back the trailer in." Without waiting for her to answer, Alex opened the driver's side door and gestured for her to climb up

"Ah, I don't know how I'd do that. I'd prefer not to."

"Nah, come on, it's easy. If you can drive a car and follow instructions, you'll be fine. Just do what I say." He grabbed her hand and gently pushed her toward the vehicle. When she stepped up, his hand brushed her butt. She pulled away from him and slammed the door. Copying the way he'd placed his elbow on the windowsill, she looked down at him. "Now what?"

"I'll get in the boat and you slowly back the truck down to the edge of the river. When I yell out, hit the brakes and the boat will slide into the water. Much safer than me standing and pushing it in." He pointed across to the other side of the narrow river. "See?"

She followed the direction in which he was pointing and gasped. Three large brown shapes, which she'd thought were logs, were sliding slowly into the water.

"Oh, my God. Are they crocodiles?"

"Yup, sure are. Good size ones, too."

"You can't get in the water. What if they—" Jess bit her lip.

"Calm down. I'll be in the boat."

"But why do you have to go on the water?"

Alex leaned in through the window and put his hand on hers. The heat burned up her arm and she shook his hand off. It must be the outback heat that was causing this stupid reaction every time he came near her.

"I'm very touched by your concern for my well-being. I'm going in the boat because I need to pull up my crab traps. It's my livelihood." Alex looked at her, and his voice was patient. "You'd hate to see a poor fisherman go without, wouldn't you?" His face was way too close to hers and he'd put his hand back on her arm.

"Go without what?" she asked waspishly.

He held her gaze and a smile played about his lips. "Go without catching fish. What else did you think I meant?"

"Oh. Go and get in your boat and get your crabs," Jess snapped. "I don't care what you do. Just do it quickly so you can get me to Cockatoo Springs and I can get my interview and go home."

"Not enjoying the trip, then?"

Did nothing upset the man?

"No, I'm not. Between you and your smart comments, your lousy driving, the heat, the dust, your smelly dog, and the whole fish thing…" She waved her arm impatiently at the boat. "I just need to do what I have to do and then everything will be okay."

Chapter Six

Alex walked to the back of the truck, whistling happily, and climbed into the boat. The trip was beginning to wear on Jess and she was getting feisty. He'd seen the sassy side of her yesterday when she'd given him the finger, and he'd wondered how long it would be before her gumption resurfaced. Grinning, he unplugged the electric cable between the boat trailer and the car, and climbed onto the trailer.

After he'd unclipped the chain securing the boat to the trailer, he called out.

"Okay, take it slow and watch me in the side mirror." Jess watched him over her shoulder as she started the truck.

"Nice and slow." Reaching down, he grabbed both sides of the boat and braced himself so he wouldn't lose his balance when the small tinny hit the water. The truck backed slowly down the slope toward the water.

He'd been teasing her about the crocodiles, but the last thing he wanted was to end up in the water. That would be taking the rough fisherman act a tad too far. Despite his constant teasing and smart remarks, and his deliberate invasion of her personal space, she'd held her cool…until now.

"Now pick up the speed a little and when I yell stop, hit the brakes." The wheels of the trailer reached the edge of the water and she slowed the truck to a crawl.

"No, not yet, go faster! Pick up the speed. Now!"

The truck stopped.

"What in the bloody hell are you doing, woman?" Casting a quick eye out for any interested crocodiles, he jumped out of the boat and ran across the sand to the cabin of the truck.

Jess looked at him without speaking.

"What are you doing? I said go fast then hit the brakes."

"I couldn't hear you," she said calmly. "And that thing…" She flicked a red-painted nail to the back of the truck. "The little house camping thingy blocked my view."

Alex rubbed the back of his neck biting down on the words of frustration he was holding back. Drawing a deep breath and releasing it before he spoke, he forced a smile onto his face and spoke patiently.

"Sorry, I'll yell a bit louder this time." He stepped up onto the running board on the side of the truck and reached in.

"Now this is what I want you to do." He

grabbed the wheel with one hand and turned it a quarter-turn to the left. "Drive back up the slope till you get to the top. You'll have to put your foot down a bit and then stop. Then we'll try again."

Jess looked at him and drove the truck back up the hill and he stayed on the running board beside her.

"Great. Stop here." He jumped down. "Now I'm going to get in the boat. What you have to remember is that the river drops off really quickly into deep water here, so when I yell stop, hit the brakes."

"Okay." Jess squared her shoulders and grasped the steering wheel with both hands. White knuckles contrasted with the red painted fingernails.

"Once the boat's in the water, drive back up to here and wait in the truck with Bowser. I've only got half a dozen traps in here, so it won't take me long to pull them out. Now that the wet is coming, I want to lift all the traps out for the season."

"Alex?" She looked at him and he couldn't decide if it was curiosity or suspicion in her expression. "How would you have done this if you'd been by yourself?"

"I would have risked the crocs. And moved bloody fast." He grinned at her. "Good money in crabs and they love them over at the chef school. Okay, all set?"

She nodded and he walked across and

climbed back into the boat.

"Okay, nice and steady." The trailer began to inch down the hill.

"Bit faster, Jess." She waved out the window and acknowledged his call, and the speed of the trailer down the riverbank increased.

"That's great, keep it going." He glanced back at the truck, caught her eye in the side mirror, and waved at her to keep going. The truck speed picked up and the wheels of the trailer hit the water.

"Okay, stop!" he yelled. "Now."

The truck stopped with a shudder and the boat slid off the trailer splashing into the river in one smooth movement. Alex reached down to start the motor as the truck roared back up the hill. A whoop came from the car. "I told you I could do anything I set my mind to."

Once the outboard had fired, he looked back up the hill Jess had parked the truck in the shade of a huge kapok tree. Her elbow was resting on the window and he gave her a thumbs up as she leaned out and grinned at him.

"That was fun. Can we do it again?"

Her cheeks were flushed and her hair was tied back with the piece of string he'd cut off for her when they'd stopped. *Didn't quite go with the designer clothes look.*

He smothered a grin. Shame she'd refused the socks. "Don't get out of the truck till I came back." His voice carried across the water and she acknowledged his words with a wave.

Alex turned the boat and headed it toward the mangroves up the river and tried to ignore the warm feeling in his chest. He'd started out to teach her a lesson, but was fast falling under her spell despite his best intentions. It would be interesting to watch when she got to Cockatoo Springs and see how long her determination held out.

Anything she set her mind to. Well, not this time.

It was good to be away from her for a while. If he wasn't careful, he was going to fall in the usual Richards' way. He'd learned the hard way with Emily and he wasn't going to be sucked in again. No matter how attractive she was.

***

Jess groaned and pushed the little dog away from her as yet another unpleasant smell wafted up to her. He snuffled in his sleep and curled up on the passenger seat. It was unbearably hot inside the truck. She tipped up her water bottle, draining the last few drops. Alex had been gone over half an hour and the temperature in the truck had risen as the sun climbed to its zenith.

"Little dog, I don't know what you've been eating, but it smells like rubber bands." It was a choice between the odour coming from the dog or the insects. A swarm of small black flies had arrived soon after Alex had disappeared around the bend, and she'd wound the window up except for a small crack at the top. They'd filled the cabin of the truck, but she'd managed to swat most of the stragglers with a rolled-up newspaper she'd found in the glove compartment. The heat was becoming unbearable and she was going to have to get out of the truck before she expired from the heat.

God, how the hell did I ever get myself into this situation?

When she'd found out she couldn't drive across to Cockatoo Springs she should have got straight back into the rental car and driven back up a real highway to the city. The date for her return flight back to New York was open, and the office was winding down for the Christmas break, so there'd been no urgency for her to get back to New York.

Reaching for Bowser's leash she picked it up and looked at the clip trying to figure out how to attach it to his collar. If they stayed well back from the water, it should be fine. She'd keep the dog close, stand near the truck, and keep her eyes open for all the other assorted venomous creatures that seemed to inhabit this country. No matter how small her apartment was at home, and how much traffic she had to battle every day to get into Manhattan, it was what she loved.

Despite what Alex had instructed, she

couldn't stay in the truck a minute longer. Nor could the dog—he'd die of heat exhaustion as well. He said he wasn't going to be gone for long, and he'd been gone for ages. Jess clipped the leash onto the dog's collar and cursed as she lost another fingernail in the process.

"Shit," she muttered. "Please, somebody take me to a nice hotel room with a real bathroom, and air conditioning…and a manicurist."

Opening the door, she waved with one hand as the cloud of black flies descended before she'd even swung her legs out. Balancing carefully on the running board beneath the open door, she scanned the ground for snakes.

All clear.

Grabbing the dog under her arm, she stepped down to the fine white sand and groaned as a drop of slobber soaked through her silk top.

Look on the bright side. At least it's cool.

As soon as they were on the ground, she bent down and looked under the side of the truck, in case anything was sheltering from the hot sun. She didn't want any surprises jumping out and grabbing her leg. Walking around the front of the truck, she found a patch of deep shade close to the huge trunk of the tree and leaned against the smooth bark and closed her eyes for a moment. The air moved slightly, and she took a deep breath appreciating the cooler breeze as Bowser sat patiently at her feet.

Her eyes flew open and she turned when something soft and feathery brushed against her cheek. She jumped back with a soft scream. A huge, pale-green praying mantis had a half-eaten brown moth between its pincers had landed on the tree trunk beside her face and was slowly devouring the moth's head. Jess shuddered and turned away just as the low hum of an outboard motor drifted across to her.

Thank God.

Before she could move, Bowser pulled on the leash and it dropped from her hand. With a screech, Jess ran after him. Forgetting all about snakes and prickles, and paying no regard to the ground beneath her flimsy sandals, she chased him toward the water and the oncoming boat.

"Bowser!" She screamed as the dog ran down the bank into the water and began yapping at the boat and his master.

"Shit. Bowser, get back." The more Alex yelled, the louder the dog yapped. "Jess, you stop right there. Don't you come any closer to the water."

There was no way she was going to be responsible for the little dog ending up in the jaws of a man-eating crocodile, no matter how bad he smelled or slobbered.

Kicking off her sandals, she ran down the sloping sand into the water and scooped the little dog up in her arms. A huge swirl in the water just out from the edge broke the surface and Jess froze, unable to move. Alex gunned the motor and the small aluminium boat whizzed across the river and over the spot where the water had swirled only seconds before. The boat roared onto the shore at full speed, scraped along the sandy bottom, and wedged on the sand beside them. He cut the motor and jumped out and grabbed her, pushing her and Bowser up the sandy bank.

"Jeez, Jess, are you okay?" He spoke quietly as if not to spook her any more than she'd already been. He wrapped his arms around her and held her tightly against his chest as she began to shake uncontrollably.

Burying her face into his chest, she nodded. "I'm sorry. I just couldn't bear the thought of him being eaten. I know I wasn't supposed to get out of the truck, but it was too hot in there." Her voice was muffled in his soft T-shirt, and she couldn't help but notice his chest was rock hard. His heart thudded against her cheek and she closed her eyes. "Thank you."

"You might be a city slicker pain in the ass, but I wasn't going to let you get eaten by a crocodile."

She didn't move for a minute, appreciating the strength of the arms holding her.

"Jess?"

Alex was looking down at her intently, his blue eyes narrowed. She held his gaze and her heart began to race as he lowered his head. She couldn't move, and she watched fascinated as his lips came closer. They were a mere breath away, and Bowser yapped at her feet, interrupting them.

"I'm okay now, thanks." Pushing away, she walked to the top of the bank and picked up her sandals before going across to the truck.

She opened the door, climbed in, and slammed it behind her, taking deep breaths as she willed her thudding heart to slow down. Alex followed her and opened the other door and put Bowser on the seat next to her. The dog came across the seat and snuggled into her, obviously sensing her distress. A warm wet tongue scraped along the side of her face and she laughed shakily.

"That was a stupid thing to do, Bowser," she said. "You nearly got us both eaten."

Alex watched them through the open door. "You've made a buddy there. He doesn't usually take to other people."

Jess looked up from the dog to Alex. Perspiration ran down the side of his face and his shirt was damp. He held her gaze and her uncertainty was reflected in his eyes. She looked away as a shaft of warmth sent another shake through her body, but this time it wasn't fear making her legs weak.

***

Alex cursed himself as he headed back to the boat.

Christ, his stupid game of showing her up could have ended in tragedy. All she'd been doing was trying to look after his dog, and she could have ended up as crocodile bait. He'd seen some close calls over the past seven years, but that had been the worst.

What sort of idiot was he? Teaching her a lesson in honesty was one thing, but putting her in danger?

No more.

He'd put his head down and focus on getting them to Cockatoo Springs with no more incidents, and then he'd sort her out once they'd arrived safely. She could stay for a holiday, but he wasn't going to break and give in to an interview. He'd taken the job under sufferance, he'd built the school up faster than anyone had anticipated, but that was as far as it went. He was getting out soon, and Alessandro Ricardo was going to disappear for good. No matter how much Jess wanted to get a scoop and publicise it, his private life was private.

Not negotiable.

She could interview Mitch and get the information second hand if it meant she'd get a job out of it. He still didn't know whether she was being truthful, and once they got to Cockatoo Springs he wasn't going to stick around to find out.

Jess sat quietly next to him cradling Bowser on her lap while he backed the trailer to the water, and hooked the boat on. He drove back up the slope and parked beneath the stand of melaleucas, and then transferred the crabs into the iced cooler in the back of the truck.

"Just going to check the forecast, and then we'll have a cuppa and head off." He held up the satellite phone to Jess and she gave him a brief smile before he walked around the back of the boat and called Mitch, his assistant manager at Cockatoo Springs.

"Where are you, Alex?" Mitch's voice was muffled by the connection. "Clay's arrived."

"Just turned off the main road, I'm taking the shortcut across."

"Why? A bit risky with the rain coming."

"Long story, mate. I'll tell you when I get there. If I need help if the river comes up, I'll radio in and you can send the chopper out. Got a good haul of crabs for you, and the barramundi went to Darwin last night."

Mitch laughed. "It's already here. Clay checked and got it in fresh before they could freeze it. He's got the first class doing it today."

"Great stuff. I can't wait to meet him."

Alex ended the call and lifted the small cooler out of the boat, and walked over to the truck. Unzipping the canvas, he reached in and pulled the old blanket from the back.

Might as well give Jess somewhere to sit. She'd been very quiet since the episode on the water. He spread it on some soft grass well back from the river before going over and opening the door to the truck. Jess looked at him and anticipation filled her voice.

"Are we leaving now?

"Soon. Come and have something to eat and then we'll head off for the last leg. I hope." He was going to be honest about what was ahead. "I want to stop and get our camp set up before dark. It's raining up ahead.

"How do you know?"

"I was talking to my…to my mate at Cockatoo Springs. Rains started over on the coast last night so we're going to have to be careful."

Jess rolled her eyes at him as she stepped out of the truck. "Whatever. Can't get much worse, can it?"

Alex shook his head as she strode ahead of him to the blanket.

Oh yes, it can. If the rains start, we are going to get stranded on this back road and I don't know if I could handle being stranded in the outback with you for too long.

She had determination in bucket loads. He was enjoying her quick comebacks, and although she'd bitched about the heat and the dog amongst other things, she was giving it a go.

When he'd held her after she'd saved Bowser, a feeling, long-buried, had shimmied up into his chest, and he hadn't liked it one bit. Jess was playing havoc with his emotions, and he was angry at himself for putting himself into that situation. But the longer they travelled and the more he threw at her, the more respect he was developing for her toughness.

Even though she'd headed off in the wrong direction on her journey and ended up with him, she was coping despite everything he'd thrown at her. Even when he'd deliberately invaded her personal space and pressed up against her, she'd only looked at him and not commented. But that wasn't going to happen again, anyway, getting up close and personal with her was not an option. He was going to stay well clear. She was way too appealing and he wasn't going to go there.

Jess lifted the blanket carefully and looked around the edge of the grassed area before she flopped down onto the ground next to him.

"Don't worry, I've already checked for snakes. Just watch out for those grass seeds I told you about." He held up the flask. "I'm sorry…no coffee. I've only got tea. Wally's missus puts the tea leaves in the flask and it's pretty strong, but it will quench your thirst."

"What do you do up here all year?" Jess looked at him over the mug of tea she'd accepted.

"In the off season, I do a bit of this and that around Cockatoo Springs. Sometimes I help with the tours." He looked at her. "There's a really good trip you should take if you stay there long enough. It's a trip out into the bush, gathering bush foods, and learning about bush tucker."

Her face lit up with interest and his stomach clenched. She was altogether too beautiful for his peace of mind. Even with her hair tied back with a piece of string and his old fishing shirt buttoned up to her throat.

"That sounds fabulous. I've never read about that. I could include it in my article." She tipped her head to the side and held his gaze. "Have you always fished up here? No other career?"

Alex looked up as the flock of red-tailed cockatoos squealed overhead. Something had disturbed them—he looked around to see what had set them off, but couldn't see anything around. He turned his attention back to Jess. Her mug was beside her and she'd sprawled out on the blanket on her stomach with her chin propped in her hands.

It wouldn't hurt to be truthful here.

"I came to the Territory two years ago."

"Where from?"

"A small town called Armidale in the middle of New South Wales."

"No fishing there?"

"No, not this sort of fishing. I grew up in the country, and I'd never held a fishing rod until I went out on a charter from Darwin and I was hooked. Pardon the pun.

"So, what did you do before that?"

"I studied to be an environmental lawyer and worked for the government in Brisbane for a while." Alex held her gaze in his and shrugged. "At least I ended up here, working in the environment."

"That's a big change. What made you leave law?"

He stared off into the distance and the raucous noise kicked up by the cockatoos stopped as suddenly as it had started.

"Life happened. I needed a change."

"Law wasn't for you?"

"Family circumstances."

He'd left Emily behind in the cemetery on that cold hill in Armidale and hadn't talked about her since he'd come to the Territory. Not only had he had to deal with her death, but her betrayal had screwed with his head and his emotions for the first year. He'd only started to move on these past few months.

"You're quiet." Jess rolled over and sat up, placing her hand on his arm. "And you have a sad look on your face. I hope I haven't upset you."

She chewed her lip looking across at him

with concern

Feelings he hadn't let surface for years were filling his chest. He dropped his head and pulled Bowser over onto his lap.

"I have two brothers and three sisters. I'm the baby of the family. My two brothers, even though they are very different in personality, both disagree with how I handled a situation a couple of years back." Alex laughed shortly, but there was no amusement in it. "Nick and Tom both think I ran away from home, and they can't understand me giving up my law career." He looked up at the sky and lifted one hand.

"But hey, they were wrong. It's not all about money." He gestured around them. "Look what I have. The outback has looked after me, and I'm pretty damn happy. I haven't done too badly up here."

As soon as his contract finished in the next couple of weeks, he had to figure out what he was going to do with the rest of his life. But first, he had to sort out his passenger.

Chapter Seven

The raw pain in Alex's voice when he talked about the 'situation,' which had been the catalyst for him coming to the Top End, piqued Jess's interest. Even though she was a food journalist, she was always interested in people, and thoughts of using Alex's story as a second article played around in her mind.

He had offered that I interview him instead of Ricardo. I could do a series seeing I've come all this way.

She was curious about what had happened to spur him onto such a dramatic move in his life, but until he volunteered the information, she wasn't going to press him.

"Did you practise law for long?" She tipped her head to the side and looked at him thoughtfully. "How old are you, Alex?"

"I worked in the government department for a while, not in a law firm. I'll be twenty-eight in a few days."

His answer surprised her; she'd picked him as a bit older than her. The tanned skin and the shaggy hair had obviously contributed to her incorrect assumption.

She smiled. "So will I. What date?

"December tenth."

"You just beat me. And we're the same age..."

"This is where a gentleman would come straight back and say 'but I thought you were only twenty-one.'" He grinned at her. "Having a birthday bash?"

If her father had his way, there would be the full blown, ridiculous extravaganza at *Spago* in Los Angeles or one of the other restaurants where he and his latest bimbo could be photographed for some ritzy magazine. Although probably not— he wouldn't want anyone to know he had a grown-up daughter.

And her mother would be in a health spa somewhere in Europe, and wouldn't even remember it *was* her birthday. Jess had called her a few days before she'd left for Australia and her mother's personal secretary answered and told her she was in the Swiss mountains. Her mother had never gotten over her father's desertion, and even though she received a healthy settlement, she'd spent most of it to trying to recapture her lost youth.

"Jess?"

"Oh, sorry. No, no party. Maybe a dinner out with my friends, Monica and Gareth, in New York if she's still talking to me after this fiasco of a trip." She held her hands out in front of her and frowned at the state of her manicure. "Poor Monica tries to keep me organised. If she could see me now, she'd die… that is, after she'd killed me first. What about you? Do you have anything big planned? Or does the outdoor life not give you time for that sort of thing?"

Alex looked at her for a moment before he answered and she could almost see the wheels turning in his head.

"My family is coming for my birthday. They're not happy I don't make the effort to go home, so they all descend on the resort for a week or so every December."

"All of them?"

"Yes." He nodded and smiled.

She'd never had much of a family life and his family sounded fascinating. If they were staying there, someone obviously had money because it was a five-star resort, and she'd seen it featured in those coffee table books with photographs of the best resorts in the world.

Alex laughed and she gazed back at him. When he smiled, the ruggedness of his face softened. "Anyway, that's enough about me…you've got the potted Alex Richards' history now. I'll shout you a birthday drink before you go back to the States. How long are you planning to stay?"

"Until after the interview with Alessandro Ricardo."

He frowned at her and suddenly she wondered if any help he could give her would be worthwhile.

"It sounds like you know a few people at the resort," she said slowly. "Tell me what you know about Ricardo."

"He's a very private person. Look, Jess. I'll be honest. When you get there, you really should just have a break and forget the idea. He doesn't do interviews. Just forget about it and have a holiday."

"You say you don't know him, so how do you know that? Maybe the right person hasn't come along yet."

There was no way she was going to give up after all she'd done to get this far.
She was going to get that interview, and if Alex couldn't help her, she'd find someone else who could.

Without answering her, Alex stood and brushed the crumbs from his shirt. Bowser sniffed around the blanket and licked them up.

"Come on. We'd better hit the road." He held his hand out to Jess and she let him pull her up. Bowser wound between her legs and she lost her balance. Alex caught her and she came up hard against his chest. Laughing self-consciously to cover the heat surging through her, she pushed him away.

"Sorry, I seem to be making a habit of falling into your arms. Don't get the wrong idea."

Alex folded up the blanket and passed it to her before lifting the cooler onto his shoulder.

"Partner back in New York?"

"Nah. No way. Career woman to the core. Had one close call, but I found out just in time he was only after—"

"After?" Alex looked at her curiously.

"After an introduction to the boss," she said. "Um, he was after a job."

"Sounds like a low life. Using a woman to get what he wanted."

They were both quiet as they walked back to the truck. Alex seemed to be lost in his thoughts as much as she was lost in hers.

Five minutes later they were back on the red dirt road and heading west. The sun was blindingly bright through the insect-smeared windscreen. Jess reached down to her bag for her sunglasses.

"Could you pass me mine please?" Alex asked. "They're in—"

"The glove compartment..." Jess finished off for him. "The never-ending glove compartment."

Jess relaxed and leaned back into the seat. "Well, I'm going to start planning my strategy for pinning down the elusive Mr. Ricardo. Oh no!"

She sat bolt upright in the seat before dropping her face in her hands and groaning. "Oh shit."

Alex hit the brakes and slowed the car looking across at her and his brow wrinkled. "What's wrong?"

"I meant to call Cockatoo Springs when I got to Daly River to make my reservation, but the rain and having to stay there for the night totally put it out of my head."

Alex started the truck again and pulled out onto the road. "No problem. You can stay at my cabin."

Why did he find that so amusing? She ignored the sexy smile on his face which made the laugh lines fan deep around his eyes.

"I can show you around."

Before Jess could answer there was a loud crack from behind them and the car slewed to the right. Alex hit the brakes and stuck his head out the window looking behind.

***

"Bloody hell." Frustration and anger warred in Alex's chest as he slammed his hands on the steering wheel. He took a deep breath and turned to Jess. "Sorry."

"What's wrong? Did we hit something?"

"There's something wrong with the boat trailer. The boat's hanging off it." He opened his door and walked back to the trailer. The two wheels were sitting at an angle, and the under frame of the boat trailer was sitting in the red dirt of the road.

"Shit." He kicked the tyre and walked around to Jess's window. "The axel of the trailer has snapped."

"How come?"

"All the corrugations on the road," he said. He should have taken it slower, but he'd been too interested in her conversation and hadn't paid enough attention to his driving. That could be deadly in the Top End. He was lucky it was only the trailer that had been damaged.

"What does that mean?"

"It means I'll have to leave the boat here."

"Won't someone steal it?" Jess pushed her door open and climbed down.

"Not in the condition it's in now. Come give me a hand and we'll be quicker."

Bowser jumped out of the truck and ran to the side of the road while Jess followed Alex around to the back of the truck. He pointed to the axel.

"We'll have to unload the boat and put as much of the gear in the back of the truck as we can. Especially the food and the crabs. Sorry, the crabs are going to have to go in the front with us. There's not enough air circulating in here, and if I unzip the windows your bed will be full of red dust for the night."

"In the cabin with the two by eighty air con?" Jess grinned up at him and his heart lurched. Last night in Janet's restaurant he'd thought how beautiful she was, but now, her clear almond-shaped eyes held his and his heart lurched.

No way, not going there.

He turned away from her and spoke gruffly. "I've just got to take the motor off the boat, and then I'll get you to help me pull the trailer off the road." Alex wiped his hands on his jeans before he lifted the side of the boat trailer.

"Will you have to come back and get it?"

"If I don't, it'll get swept away in the wet."

Her eyes were wide. "Do you mean this road will go under water?"

"Yes. For most of the summer."

Alex was looking forward to the camp ahead. It was going to be an interesting night. "You grab Bowser and get back in the truck, I'll zip this up. And then we'll get on the way. I don't want to get to our campsite too late." Huge thunderheads were spiralling up ahead, and he didn't like the look of the sky at all.

***

The first cloud covered the sun as they turned into the road to the camp. There were a couple of places they could have camped out, but Alex had chosen this one because it was on the highest ground. If there was a storm, they'd be dry up here.

He frowned as he slowed the truck. Jess was determined to go on with the interview and he'd seen her persistence over the past twenty-four hours. If she was that persistent at Cockatoo Springs, she'd figure how who he was in no time at all. He guarded his privacy fiercely and he was going to have to handle this very carefully. As soon as he got a chance, he was going to call Mitch and make sure there was no room for her at the resort when they arrived. She could stay in the spare room in the small cabin at the back of the resort where he stayed when he was hauling fish. That way he could keep her close and keep tabs on what she was doing. He wouldn't go anywhere near his beachfront villa this time—not until she was on her way back home.

Alex pulled the car to the side of the road, and looked across at Jess and Bowser. She was dozing with her head back on the seat, and her feet on top of the cooler holding the crabs. Bowser was curled up on her once-white pants, and Jess had the fingers of one hand tucked loosely into his collar, holding him secure. Her pants were streaked with red dirt and her silk top was dotted with water spots where perspiration had soaked in. Her hair was still tied back with the piece of string, but had loosened, and her topknot was hanging to one side. Her right hand was braced on the seat between them. He looked down and grinned. Two long manicured red nails, and two snapped off with chipped nail polish, completed the picture of a dishevelled traveller. If she turned up at the reception desk of his five-star resort looking like that, eyebrows would be raised.

"Jess, wake up." He touched her hand lightly. She opened her eyes and stretched, and his mouth dried as the silk top pulled across her breasts. She was almost as tall as he was, and even though she was very slim, her breasts were full. The damp silk top strained across them tightly, and she crossed her arms across her chest and glared at him.

"I have to get out and turn the wheel hubs before I can put the truck into four-wheel drive. There's just a short distance to go to where we'll camp out tonight."

Jess unfolded her arms and looked out the window. "Rain's coming?"

"Not yet." He pointed up the hill. "There's a spring-fed freshwater pool where we can wash. It's away from the main river, and there are no crocodiles there.

"I'd kill for a wash now, and before we leave in the morning so I don't turn up looking like a hobo. I was thinking too… could I use your satellite phone to make a reservation? How long will you stay there?" Jess looked at him and Alex focused on manoeuvring the truck over the deep corrugation.

The driver's side dipped to the right, and Bowser rolled along the seat and landed in his lap. Jess gasped as the car tilted back the other way at the opposite angle, and she grabbed for Bowser as he rolled back toward her. It was likely he'd be at Cockatoo Springs for a couple of weeks. He had to make time to meet with Clay, the new chef, and to work out the program for the wet season. He also had a CEO from one of the big travel companies flying in for a two-day visit. He'd been difficult and insisted on dealing with Alessandro himself, and Mitch had talked Alex into the meeting with Larry Bartholomew before he left. Then the whole family was arriving in a few days for his birthday. Last year, they'd managed to keep his fake identity secret, and although they couldn't understand his motivation, he'd never confided Emily's deception to anyone else. He had this stupid idea it was gallant to keep her memory untarnished. If he'd known how hard it would be to run the place privately once the school had taken off, he would never have even taken the job on in the first place.

The next challenge was to keep it quiet for one more visit and then once his contract was done, Ricardo could disappear quietly.

"Ah… I'll stay a week or so and then I'll head to Darwin for the wet season.

You can still fish up there away from the rivers." He had to get Jess sorted and on her way home well before his family descended. And somehow, he had to convince her that an interview with Ricardo was out of the question. Then he had to get rid of this bloody fascination she was weaving over him.

It was safe here. No crocodiles. It was time to put another plan in place and turn back into the fishing hobo who pushed her buttons. He'd been way too accommodating and he wasn't happy with this connection that seemed to be springing up between them.

***

Jess gripped Bowser with one hand and held onto the bar on the dashboard with the other. The slope Alex was driving down was so steep; she was worried the pickup would tip over its front. Her legs were jammed between the large dark blue cooler on the floor on the passenger side, and the constant clicking coming from inside the cooler was unnerving.

"What *is* that noise?" She turned to Alex who was peering over the front of the dashboard at the drop below as he turned the wheel inch by inch.

"What noise?"

"That clicking noise."

"Oh, that's the crabs. As soon as we stop, I need to get them sorted. I didn't have time to tie them up, and some had already thrown their nippers. They'll be our dinner tonight."

"Oh, okay." Jess turned away as an idea formed in her mind. "Alex?"

"Yes?" His voice was patient, but he didn't take his eyes off the terrain ahead as he reached down and changed down a gear. A loud grinding sound came from beneath the gear shift.

"Shit, that doesn't sound good." The speed of the truck picked up and he planted his boot on the brake pedal."

"What's wrong?" she asked.

"Sounds like we just did a gear." He cocked his head to the side and listened as he changed gears again. "Maybe not. I'll check when we stop." He gingerly lifted his foot off the brake pedal and changed down another gear, and the car still slowed. "Don't worry, it's okay. We're almost down to the clearing."

Jess turned and looked out the window. The road was narrow and the branches of the low shrubs were scraping against the glass.

"Oh, my God." She gulped, closing her eyes as a huge brown snake slid back into the bush beside the pickup.

"What did you say?"

"Nothing." Jess turned and scowled at him. "I cannot wait to get to the resort." She held out her hand and ticked off on her fingers. "I really don't know what's worse. Snakes? Flies? Crocodiles? Crabs? This old clunking pickup?" She put her head into her hands, and her temper fired as Alex looked down at Bowser and spoke in a conversational tone.

"At least you're off the list now, little man."

His tone got under her skin. "Please tell me this resort is really five stars and not one of those wilderness lodges where the guests are expected to rough it and enjoy themselves."

The smarter her mouth got, the more he smiled.

"No, everything Madame could possibly require is catered for at Cockatoo Springs." He pointed to her broken fingernails. "I believe there is a day spa where they do hair and nails...and massage. The rooms are luxurious, and of course the food in the restaurant is world class. But I forgot that's all you are interested in, isn't it?" He narrowed his eyes. "What will you do if you can't get a room? Will you catch the helicopter straight out, or will you stay at my cabin?"

Jess paused before she answered, sensing there was more to his question than just interest in her movements. "Of course I'm not going to leave. If can't get a room, I'll be very grateful for your offer, thank you. But I'm sure there'll be a room."

"I'll call my mate as soon as we're unpacked. Anyway, look." He pointed ahead. "We're finally here."

Chapter Eight

"Oh, my God. This is paradise." Jess opened the door, and the little dog jumped up beside her. "What about Bowser, does he need his leash?"

God, I can't believe I'm worried about a dog.

The heat in the Top End was turning her brains to mush, as well as her usually impeccable grooming. There was no word for how she looked…and felt. She reached up and pulled the string from her hair, shaking it all out, and regretted it immediately. Even though the sun was low in the sky, the heat was still unbearable.

"He's okay. There are no crocs here. I'll keep an eye on him. He won't wander far from me or the truck."

Jess slid out of the truck and stepped to the edge of the low bluff, looking nervously at the ground.

"Don't worry, as soon as the truck came in, any snakes would have taken off. If you leave them alone and don't provoke them, they'll leave you alone."

Jess forgot all about snakes as she looked over the edge of the drop. Water cascaded down the face of the rock in front of her to a deep green pool fringed with trees. The storm clouds had receded, and the late afternoon shade covered the western end of the pool. The water beneath the rock face below them sparkled invitingly as the cascading water hit the surface of the pool. Alex walked over and stood behind her.

"I love the Top End. There are hundreds more places like this, all off the tourist track and pristine."

"It sounds like the environmentalist is still in there."

"Nah, just someone who appreciates nature at its best. Now come on, let's get organised and then we can have a dip."

"Don't forget to use the phone and call about my booking."

"Right. I'll go and do that now."

Alex went around to the back of the truck and Jess waited at the edge of the bluff enjoying the view. All was quiet and when he reappeared, he held up the phone with a grim expression.

"Sorry, the battery's flat. I'll have to charge it up."

"How can you do that? I suppose there's a hidden power outlet in the glove compartment along with everything else." She tried to be flippant to cover the disappointment of not being able to contact the resort, and find out if her room had been held for her.

"Almost," Alex said. "There's an inverter in the back of the track."

Jess had no idea what he was talking about so she ignored him and looked out over the water. Perspiration trickled down her neck as they unpacked the truck, and she looked down ruefully at her ruined silk shirt. Alex carted the cooler from the cab of the truck and placed it in the shade beneath an overhanging rock. The heat was vicious, even hotter than last night. She'd thought the air conditioning in her room at the Daly River caravan park had malfunctioned because it had been so hot in there.

Maybe it was this hot in the outback all the time?

"Does it get any cooler through the night?" She swatted a fly away as Alex walked back to the truck for the next load.

"Not a lot." He frowned at her. "Jess, go and get the Bushman's out of the glove compartment. Not only are those black files annoying, but the midges will bite you. And the mosquitoes carry disease up here."

Jess shivered at the thought of something sucking her blood. She hurried over to the truck and pulled herself up on the passenger side. Alex had parked it awkwardly between two boulders, and backed it in as close as he could to the large cliff face behind it, leaving just enough room to get into the canvas tent on the back of the truck. The driver's side was lower, and she slid in through the narrow space between the door and the rock. She reached across to the seat before opening the glove compartment and poking around.

Of course. The first thing to fall into her hand was the box of condoms.

Well, he won't be needing them this trip. She shoved them to the back of the compartment and peered in. A small light green plastic bottle proclaiming Bushman's in red writing was jammed at the back of the space. She pulled it out and read the label:

Guaranteed fifteen hours of protection. That should just about see her out of this place and back into a civilised environment. Although, if she was honest, it was one of the most beautiful places she'd ever seen. She couldn't wait to get into that pool down on the rock platform.

After closing the compartment, Jess climbed out of the door and looked carefully down to the ground before walking around to the back of the truck. She'd find her swimsuit first, and then lather herself in this lotion.

Straining to reach the zipper to undo the back door, she cursed as she snapped another fingernail.

"Can't reach?" The amused voice came from behind her. "Step back. I'll climb in and pass some of the stuff out to you. I'll throw down the heavy stuff."

Alex reached up, unzipped the heavy metal zipper, and hoisted himself into the back of the truck. Jess peered in and got an eyeful of taut butt in snug fitting denim jeans. Heat ran up her neck and added to her already overheated state. She fanned herself, but it only moved the heavy hot air a little and didn't cool her at all. She blinked to remove the perspiration from her eyes; the back of the truck and Alex's butt blurred. Closing her eyes, she hoped desperately that a room would be ready and waiting for her tomorrow. A nice cool bath, clean clothes, and food were what she desperately needed. She'd had nothing to eat all day apart from the muffin when they'd headed off at dawn. No wonder she was hot and weak. She'd had no idea that driving on these treacherous outback roads would be so slow.

"Whoa, Jess. Are you okay? You're as white as a sheet." She opened her eyes. Alex turned around and was leaning out of the back of the truck, looking at her with concern.

"Just need something to eat. I'm okay."

He reached into the cooler, and passed her a bottle of water and a trail mix bar before he pointed to a small boulder beside the pickup.

"You sit there while I unpack."

Gratefully, she took the water and the snack, holding the cool bottle to her cheek. She wandered over to the rock and plonked herself down. Too late, she remembered she didn't even look for snakes…or scorpions…or crocodiles. Sipping on the water, she watched Alex unload the back of the truck. He pulled everything to the back of the canopy, and again she appreciated the view as he climbed backwards out of the pickup. He reached up and lifted her suitcase, and the muscles in his arm flexed as he lowered the bag to the ground beside the truck

"What have you got in the there? Rocks?"

"Ha ha, very funny. Just clothes. I have to look the part when I do the interview."

Alex turned to her and his gaze travelled up her dirty clothes and to her overheated face and tangled hair. "Ah, yes, mustn't forget the interview."

When everything was unpacked and on the ground beside the truck, he climbed down and made two trips across to the shaded area beneath an overhanging rock.

Jess finished the water, unwrapped the trail mix, and wandered over to where Alex was setting up their camp. "Can I help?" She looked curiously at a long canvas bag next to the cooler. "What's that?"

"That's my swag."

"Your what?"

"It's a combination of a bed, a tent, and a sleeping bag. All rolled up into one compact little bag. Haven't you ever been camping?"

Jess grinned at him and shook her head as she munched on the trail mix. "No… I didn't even go to summer camps when I was a kid. My father—"

He looked at her waiting for her to finish.

"Nothing," she said not wanting to talk about her father. It was too nice an afternoon to start thinking about him, and the way he'd treated her when she was growing up. Alex looked at her curiously as he gathered a pile of sticks and brush together. Jess wandered over and sat next to the circle of rocks he'd set up around the makeshift fireplace.

"My father thought camping was a bit ordinary. He preferred to give me what he called enriched experiences. So we went to art galleries, museums, and spent a lot of time in places where he could be seen." She sighed and wiped her forehead with the back of her arm.

"I know a lot about art, and old bones, but nothing about the outdoors." She laughed. "I also didn't know a lot about the Outback. I don't know if I would have come if I'd known what it was going to be like."

Alex stood beside her, his arms full of bits of wood. "Even for the chance of getting the scoop interview for your magazine?"

"Even for the interview." She shook her head and looked down at her clothes. "Look at me. I was totally unprepared for this."

"Well." He dropped the wood to the ground and squatted next to her. "As a fair dinkum Aussie, I'd better give you a better impression of the outback. What do you say about a swim?"

Despite the petulant expression on her grimy face, Alex was surprised by his need to keep looking at her. There was some sort of chemistry in action, and she fascinated him. He'd obviously been away from women too long, and he'd have to get out his little black book out when he got back to Darwin. He'd been missing out on that part of male-female relationships lately.

That's all it was. Nothing to do with finding her so bloody attractive.

"What are you thinking about?" she asked. "You've got a funny look on your face."

Caught out fantasizing about taking her to bed, or rather to his swag, Alex cleared his throat. He stood and held his hand out to her. She grabbed it and he pulled her up, ignoring the warmth of her hand in his. "Come on, we'll go for a swim and then I need to cook you a decent meal."

Alex looked down at her hand. Her fingers somehow had got entwined through his. Slowly he lifted his gaze up to her face. She'd pulled her hair back and retied it with the string and left her face unframed. Her clear green eyes were fixed on their joined hands and the blood rushed straight to his groin.

"Ready to swim?" he asked softly, ignoring the pulsing in his jeans.

Surprise flickered in her face when she glanced up at him. She didn't have to look up far; she was only a few of inches below his six three even in her flat sandals.

All rational thought had fled, and her lips beckoned his as she held his gaze steadily, her clear green eyes assessing him, and filled with the knowledge that she knew exactly what he was thinking.

Her lips parted a little and he dropped his head, capturing them beneath his. Her hands wound around his neck and he pulled her closer to him. Her mouth opened and he groaned, unable to help himself anymore, losing himself in the sweet depths. He lifted his hand and held her face gently while he deepened the kiss. Jess caught her breath on a soft gasp as his teeth scraped hers, and his tongue began a slow seductive dance with hers. His mind was just beginning to haze like the heat shimmering over the far horizon when she drew back and looked up at him

"And what was that all about it?" she asked.

"I needed to."

She reached down and held his hand up to her face, taking time to examine it, and he sensed she was avoiding his gaze. He tilted her chin up with the fingers that were resting against the side of her face.

"Was I out of line?" he asked, willing her to look up at him. When she held his gaze, lazy desire swirled in his chest. Although she didn't meet his gaze, he could see the smile playing about her lips.

"No, I'm a big girl now." Finally, she lifted her head and met his eyes, and the jolt that hit his chest almost took his breath away.

"I can take care of myself. But I don't know that I was quite expecting this."

Her face told him a different story. A soft flush sat on her high cheekbones and her lips were slightly open when she looked back at him, tempting him, but he dropped her hand. He turned away, trying to push away the need to take her in his arms and continue where they'd left off.

Too complicated. He didn't need any complications in his life.

Chapter Nine

Jess scrabbled around in her suitcase willing her heart to stop beating so fast.

It was the heat. She was dehydrated. She had a lot to worry about. It was her job.

It had nothing to do with this rough and hard fisherman, who had just taken her to heaven for a brief moment with his mouth. She glanced at him as he moved the coolers further into the shade of the overhanging rock. He was tough, and strong, and his face was rugged and unshaven, but his mouth had been soft and inviting, and he had taken her by surprise. Now all she could think about was getting up closer to him and trying it again.

No way. One night, and she'd be back in civilisation and doing the job she came here to do. She was *not* going to get side tracked. Imagine the text she could send Monica.

In the bush. Smelly fisherman. Great sex.

Because she knew it would be great sex. He had that lean whipcord, masculine body. His hands were strong and his hair was begging to be gripped while he—

"Jess?"

She jumped and smiled, drawn out of her fantasy. Pulling her swimsuit from her suitcase, she shoved everything back in, ignoring the red dust that was everywhere. She shook the dust from her swimsuit and looked around at him.

"Where can I change?"

He grinned back at her and then slowly turned around, putting his back to her. Jess let her gaze wander over his broad shoulders and the snug-fitting faded jeans encasing his butt.

"Right where you're standing." He stood waiting, and she figured he would be a gentleman. She undressed quickly, pulling on the sleek black swimsuit with the plunging neckline. Shivers ran down her back and turned into heat when they reached between her thighs and stopped.

"Okay, you can turn around now," she said.

Jess grinned as Bowser barked and ran over to her. She reached down to pat him, and knew she looked good. This swimsuit had cost her a fortune and it moulded her curves in all the right places, or so the saleswoman in the exclusive boutique had said.

"Thank you, Bowser. I'll take that as a compliment."

She glanced across at Alex. A pulse flicked in his cheek and he stood still for a moment while his gaze swept from her face to her feet. He took a step toward her, and her breath hitched, but he all he did was take her hand and lead her over to the edge of the bluff.

"Come on, you're in for a treat." His voice was rough.

Keeping hold of her hand, Alex helped her down the rocky slope, and Jess tried to ignore the warmth taking over her whole body.

It's only the heat. The hot air, nothing else.

Her sandals slipped on the loose rocks and she stumbled. Alex slid his arm around her back to hold her steady, and she fought the heat that began beneath his fingers, rippled down her stomach, and lower.

She needed to cool off in the water. As soon as possible.

When they got to the bottom of the hill, Jess stood silently and drank in the vista in front of her. From above she hadn't been able to appreciate the waterfall cascading down the rock just beneath where the truck was parked. From sixty feet above, water fell in a white froth over a series of stepped rocks down to the clear, deep pool edged by pure white sand. A tall tree with lacy foliage overhung the water at the far end, its lazy movement reflected in the still green depths. The gorge walls rose high, and she had to crane her head back to see the bright blue sky.

It was cooler down here next to the water. A slight breeze puffed and ruffled the surface of the pool. Jess turned to Alex who was staring across the water.

"This is magical," she said." I had no idea it could be so beautiful just a few hundred yards away from that dusty road." She leaned over the edge of the pool and peered into the water. "But are you sure there's no crocodiles?"

Alex laughed and dropped his head, reaching for the bottom of his T-shirt.

"No. No crocodiles. I can prove it. I can walk you back and show you that it feeds from a spring a few hundred metres back in the bush. There's not even any freshies up here."

Jess walked over and sat on the side of the pool and removed her sandals. "Okay, I'll take your word for it." She leaned over and trailed her fingers in the water and looked up with surprise. "Wow, it's hot!"

"Maybe not hot, but certainly warm." Alex squatted down beside her and pointed to the far end of the pool. Jess swallowed dryly as the muscles flexed in his arm.

And pecs, and a six-pack to die for.

"It's deep enough to dive down that end. It starts shallow here at the falls and the hot rock warms the water even though it comes from underground, and then it drops off pretty quickly. It'll be much cooler down that end."

"I should have brought my soap and

shampoo down. I didn't think."

She caught Alex smiling at her.

"Go on, say how forgetful I am. I can see it on your face." Jess laughed as he shook his head.

"Never." He raised his hands in denial, and her gaze was drawn to the top of his unclipped jeans. A line of dark hair disappeared southward and her mouth was suddenly dry, again.

"I'll go up and get it. Where is it?"

"In the pink bag next to my suitcase. Just bring the bag down, thanks. It'll be luxury to have a wash in this warm water."

She turned and watched him climb back up the path. His jeans had slipped down a little, and a pair of black Calvin Klein briefs peeked over the top. The afternoon sun shone on the deeply tanned skin of his bare back.

Jess folded her arms across her breasts as she watched the taut muscles in his lean legs flex as he reached the top of the slope. When she'd climbed into his truck this morning, an interlude like this had been far from her thoughts. She'd fully expected to be checked and settled in her room at Cockatoo Springs by the end of the day.

If I have a room.

By the time he scrambled back down the path and placed her toiletries bag next to her, she had her desire under control. *Almost.* If he touched her, she was sure she'd ignite. To her relief, as soon as he'd dropped the bag beside her, Alex walked around to the far end of the pool and dropped his jeans. Jess busied herself in her bag, pulling out body wash and shampoo, and didn't look up again until she heard a splash at the far end. For a moment, there was no sign of him and then he surfaced and swam to the waterfall. Standing under the cascading water, he shook his head and tilted his head back beneath the streaming water. His hair was sleek and black, and plastered to his skull. She stared at his eyelashes, stuck together in spiky clumps around his deep blue eyes.

"Coming in? The water's beautiful."

Jess knew what would happen if she got in the water with him. It wasn't only the thought of the cool water lapping her skin that beckoned her. She swung her legs over the edge of the rock and slid in, sighing as the warm water caressed her skin. Bubbles ran up her legs as the water moved against her, and she pushed herself out to the middle to the deeper water and dived under. Opening her eyes beneath the water, she was amazed at how clear it was. She looked up and the blue sky rippled through the surface of the water above her. She surfaced and turned to face Alex as his strong hands grasped her waist.

He moved quickly, and in an instant his mouth was hot, hungry, and hard against hers. His hands held her tightly, pulling her closer, and she couldn't stop herself. She wound her legs around his hips and he groaned into her mouth. This kind of raw, primeval need was new to her. Sex was usually civilised and polite, and in a bed, after the required social preliminaries, but she responded in a way that was foreign to her. The low guttural moan that escaped her lips echoed the desire that coursed through her.

For the first time in her life, she surrendered without thought. He kissed her and she whimpered against his mouth and clutched at his shoulders.

"Okay?" He smiled down at her.

Jess nodded while she kept her gaze fixed on those dark blue eyes and wound her arms around his neck.

"It's a long walk to the glove compartment," he said roughly

"You should have thought of that box when you were getting my bag," she said playfully.

Alex dropped his forehead on hers and closed his eyes. "That would have been making a big assumption. I didn't intend for this to happen, you know."

"Neither did I." Jess pulled her head back and looked at him. "So, what are we going to do now?"

"If you keep looking at me like that, I won't think straight," he said. "How about I go back to the truck and it'll give you time to think if you really want to take up where we left—"

Jess ran her hands down the smooth tanned skin of his back as her lips cling to his. "Is that answer enough?"

"God, Jess."

She smiled and removed her arms from around him. "Okay, you go back up to the Boy Scout compartment…and I'll be waiting."

Alex dove under the water and swam across to the waterfall before he pulled himself up onto one of the rock steps beneath the cascading water. Even though her blood was zinging around her body with anticipation, she'd hadn't felt this relaxed or had as much fun since…since she couldn't remember when.

Closing her eyes, she tipped her head back and floated in the warm water, waiting for Alex to come back down the hill. The soft breeze picked up, cooling her damp cheeks and rustled the leaves of the branches overhanging the pool. The breeze dropped, but the rustling continued, and a soft grunt came from behind her. Jess opened her eyes and rolled over in the water as a frisson of fear rippled down her spine, replacing the anticipation of a moment ago. She stood, and turned slowly as the grunting got louder.

A huge black…thing…with slits for eyes and long yellowed tusks sticking from its bottom jaw stood at the edge of the pool, its dark beady eyes fixed on her. Black bristles poked through the red mud coating its massive shoulders. She watched as it strutted closer to the edge and scratched at the ground with its front feet. She gasped and moved slowly toward the other side of the pool, as far away from the massive thing as she could, while it snorted and folded its front legs under its huge bulk and dropped its snout into the water.

"Alex!" She screamed at the top of her voice and the pig lifted its head and stared at her. From the bush behind the huge boar, came a small sow and half a dozen piglets. The sow stood guard rigidly while the piglets joined their father at the edge of the shallow water.

Without removing her gaze from the creature, she reached down under the water with shaking hands, and pulled up her swimsuit as she backed into the deeper water.

Oh God. Can pigs swim?

Chapter Ten

Alex slid across the seat of the truck, the small box safely in his hand. Bowser was curled up on the floor of the pickup and opened one lazy eye before tucking his nose back under his paw.

Alex's blood ran cold when Jess screamed for him. He slammed the door of the pickup shut, and the box of condoms back through the open window. He took off at a fast run toward the rocky path until he reached the edge of the drop, looking over to see what had spooked her.

Shit.

A fat sow and seven piglets stood beside one of the biggest feral pigs he had ever seen.

"Stay in the water, Jess! Don't move. As long as you stay in the water it can't hurt you."

"Can it swim?" Her voice was shaking and she didn't take her eyes off the boar. It was huge.

Shit, just her luck to get bailed up by one. He scrambled down the rocky slope, small rocks skittering to the bottom beneath his bare feet. The boar turned and sniffed the ground. Picking up a fist-sized piece of rock, he flung it at the boar, but missed. Now at the bottom of the slope, the pig stiffened and turned toward him, snorted and dropped its head, charging for him.

Bloody hell.

Jess's scream followed him as he ran for the nearest tree. He grabbed the lowest branch and swung himself up. The tree shook as five hundred pounds of solid razorback crashed into the trunk two metres below. Just to be extra sure, Alex pulled himself up another branch before turning to the pool and checking on Jess.

She disappeared and he scanned around the pool, worried for a moment she'd climbed out the other side and was heading back up to the truck. Jess would have no idea how fast these suckers could move and how deadly they were. He let out a sigh of relief when the water rippled and Jess surfaced slowly over near the waterfall.

"Good girl, just stay over there. It can't hurt you."

"So what the hell do we do now? You're up a tree and I'm down here in the water." Her eyes were huge as she stared at the pig. "What happens next?"

"We'll have to wait it out."

"Are you serious?" Jess stood and folded her arms and flicked a glance up to him, only taking her eyes from the pig for a split second.

"Unless you want to climb out of the water and chase it away."

"No chance, buddy. You're the outback hero. That's your job."

Alex folded his arms and leaned back against the rough bark, and looked down as another snort floated up to him. But it hadn't come from the pig. Jess grinned up at him and when he looked at her she giggled again.

"Oh my God." The water splashed as she slapped her hands on top of it. "I so wish I had my camera. I could write the best article about the Aussie outback and its heroes…in their underwear."

Alex looked down at his black Calvin Kleins. "You won't find it so funny if the boar decides to settle his family in here for the night."

"Really?"

That quickly wiped the smile from her face. Alex slid down the trunk and settled in for a wait. He looked up and groaned as an avalanche of small rocks tumbled over the edge of the rock face, splashing into the water. Bowser was standing on top of the bluff, and if a dog could look happy, he would have beamed in anticipation of the fun to come. He took off into the bush, his ears flattened back and his neck muscles bunched.

"Oh, no. Make him stay up there. Send him back." Jess looked at Alex with wide eyes.

"No chance. He was bred for this—he'll be okay." Alex pulled himself up to watch the action below, hoping he was right. A little brindle bullet shot out of the bush, and before the pig could turn, Bowser had latched onto its ear. With a loud squeal, the pig shook its head, but the dog had a firm grip as his back legs stretched up.

"Look, Jess." Alex pointed to the sow and the piglets as they ran off into the bush. "Dad won't be far behind."

Bowser let go of the pig's ear and ran around in circles, yapping loudly. The pig pawed the ground half-heartedly before letting out one final snort and trotting off behind the others. Alex called Bowser over and he sat patiently beneath the tree waiting for him to come down.

"Some live outback action for you?" Alex jumped down and sauntered across to the pool. "Had enough entertainment for the afternoon?"

Jess rolled her eyes at him, before diving under the water and swimming over to the edge. Alex put his hand down and she glanced back over her shoulder before she reached up and took it.

"Are you sure they've gone?"

"Yep, they won't come back now they know our little pig hunter is here." He reached down and scratched Bowser's head.

"Great job, buddy."

Jess climbed out of the pool and let go of his hand. She reached up and squeezed the water out of her hair before walking over to collect her bag.

"What else have you got lined up for

tonight?"

###

Even though she was showing a brave face and coming out with the sassy comments, Jess was unsettled. Her legs were shaking as she followed Alex and Browser up the hill, keeping an eye out behind her for the return of the pigs. He didn't put his hand out to help her, and she didn't look for it. If she was totally honest, it wasn't the pigs that had unsettled her. The interlude in the pool with Alex had touched her deeply. A level of need she had never before experienced had tugged deep within her and she was grateful to the wild pigs for bringing it to a halt. She wasn't ready for that, and she didn't want it in her life.

They reached the top of the hill, and Bowser scampered to the shade beneath the truck. Alex strode over and reached in, pulling his jeans from the truck and casually stepping into them before he turned to Jess. Her skin was already dry from the hot tropical sun, even though it was late afternoon, and her hair was drying in a huge tangle. Alex opened the back of the pickup and gestured inside.

"Do you want to climb in here? You can get dressed and sorted while I cook the crabs."

He seemed to sense she needed some privacy and time to herself, and she smiled at him gratefully.

"Thanks, I will. But how are you going to

cook them? They're still alive."

"I'll drop them into the pot when the water boils."

"Ew, and you call yourself an environmentalist? That is so cruel."

"Yes, little Ms. Food Journalist, that's how you cook them." Alex shook his head and ran his hand down the side of her face. "Alive."

A jolt of heat ran from his fingers to his skin, and he held her gaze for a moment before he turned away and walked over to the other side of the low-burning fire to collect her suitcase. Jess unzipped the flap of the little camp house on the back of the pickup and put her cosmetics bag on the foam mattress.

"Make sure you put some of that Bushman's on and zip up the flap of the canopy. As soon as the sun sets, the mozzies will be bloody crook," he said.

She watched him tip the lotion into his hand and rub it onto his face, neck, and chest before passing the bottle to her. No matter how hard she tried, she couldn't stop her eyes following his hand as he rubbed brisk circles on his flat stomach. He was a good-looking man in prime condition, and her body reacted accordingly.

Get over it, Jess. If he chooses to walk around without a shirt, you can cope.

She clambered into the back of the pickup and wrinkled her nose. She closed up the flap. It was dim inside, and a combination of smells greeted her. The hot air was suffocating, and when she sat up straight to take a deep breath, her stomach protested, and she gagged. She pushed herself to her knees and opened her suitcase to find something clean and cool to wear. Several items of clothing were considered and discarded before she found a long silk skirt, which would protect her legs from the insects, and a spaghetti strap top with a light silk shawl to wrap around her shoulders. Dressing quickly in the small space, she ran her fingers through her curls and wound them up into a matching scarf to keep her hair away from her neck.

The memory of Alex's hands and fingers when he'd caressed her in the water shimmied through her mind, and she closed her eyes and swallowed.

One night.

One night sleeping in the back of the truck, and then some conversation tomorrow as they travelled. Then they would arrive at the resort and she'd get her room, say thank you, goodbye, and forget about him.

She could do it.

The unfamiliar feelings would be put aside and she would get on with the job and go home. She slipped on a pair of dangly earrings and a smudge of lipstick, followed by a light application of the famed Bushman's to prevent the mozzies…and the midges… and she was ready to go out and face the outback.

And Alex.

When she climbed out of the back of the pickup, the smell of garlic assailed her nostrils and she turned to the fireplace with a frown.

She must be so hungry she was imagining haute cuisine aromas.

There was no sign of Alex or Bowser, and Jess looked around nervously. The sun had set, and the lingering smoke from the grasslands fire drifted in on the light breeze. Wispy fingers of white smoke treaded thought the tops of the trees. All was quiet.

It was eerie, yet beautiful.

A flat rock next to the fire beckoned, and Jess retrieved the old blanket from the back of the truck and folded it, so it cushioned the hard rock. She sat and closed her eyes, listening to the quiet. The only sound was the occasional pop of the fire and a hiss as the water spat from the pot onto the coals. The faint sound of the waterfall sloshing in the distance added to the peace.

A few minutes later, slow footsteps and the snuffling of Bowser, announced their return.

"Sorry, Jess. I took him for a walk after I fed him, and he took off on me. Little bugger." Alex opened the door of the truck and lifted the dog into the cabin. "Are you ready to eat?"

"Yes, I'm hungry."

And not just for food.

"Wanna beer? It's all I have, sorry." Alex reached into the cooler. She held out her hand and he passed her a cold bottle before sitting across from her on the other side of the campfire. Placing the bottle against her cheek, she closed her eyes.

"What else are you cooking?"

Keep the conversation on food, you can do that without getting flustered.

"A sauce for the crab."

"And you just threw it together from what you have in the cooler? What's in it?"

"Secret ingredient. If I tell you, I'll have to kill you." Alex grinned at her and then his smile faded as he shook his head. "Oh, sorry, that was a crass thing to say. You've already had the razorback experience this afternoon. I didn't mean to be so flippant."

"You didn't scare me. Neither did the pig, really…once I knew I was safe in the water." Jess laughed and tipped her beer up appreciating the cool liquid in her dry mouth. "I enjoyed watching you climb up the tree in your—"

Whoa. Don't go there. She was trying to be nonchalant about the whole thing. If it hadn't been for the arrival of the pig, there would have been no holding either of them back. She couldn't figure him out. He said he'd been a lawyer and he was well spoken. And as much as he tried to push her buttons, she could tell that he was a good person and he'd looked out for her without hesitation when there'd been real danger Something about him being a wild fisherman in the outback just didn't make sense to her.

Alex didn't speak, but just looked at her over the fire. It was completely dark and there was no moon. The firelight flickered on his rugged face, highlighting the bluish black glints in his hair. He stood and Jess hitched a breath as heat ran through her. Alex walked over to pot and opened the cooler, placing the lid upside down on the ground. He put the cooked crabs on the lid and began to methodically shell them until a pile of steaming crabmeat filled the plate. He removed the smaller saucepan and set it next to Jess, before squatting in front of her.

"Now you are in for the treat of your life," he said softly.

Fascinated, she watched his fingers as he picked up a morsel of crab and dipped it into the sauce and held it in front of her lips.

His eyes held hers. "Hungry, Jess?"

***

A little nudge of shock ran through Alex as he held his fingers in front of Jess's mouth. Her mouth opened and the tip of her tongue ran over her lips. When he'd been walking in the scrub with Bowser, he'd been lost in his thoughts and hadn't noticed when the dog disappeared into the scrub. He was way too fascinated with this woman, and if it hadn't been for the pigs, he would have had sex with her in the pool this afternoon.

For the first time in two years, he'd lowered his defences and let his heart rule his head.

Jess was full of life, and despite being in an unfamiliar and hostile environment, she'd snapped back no matter what he'd thrown at her. Now it was time to put some distance between them Once they reached Cockatoo Springs, he had to make sure she didn't find out who he really was, and he also had to find some way to ease her disappointment at not getting the interview she'd come for.

Still, he couldn't understand it. She had the best of everything. Her clothes were top class, and she'd not given a second thought to leaving the hire car at Daly River. If she really needed a job that badly, she was throwing a lot of money around. Flying down under just on the chance of getting an interview.

She'd tried on the crazy story about being an actress last night, and maybe the food journalist story was a sham as well. Who knew what she was doing? Now he had to try to push away the heat that pulsed through him when she'd parted her soft, pink lips, ready to take the crab and the sauce off his fingers.

She leaned toward him and her lips touched

his fingers, and he was lost. He was hungry for more than the crab. She'd lit a fire in him this afternoon and it roared back to life again as her lips circled his finger.

"Mmm." She pulled back and closed her eyes. "Garlic…and chili? What's that wonderful flavour? Crab?"

Alex turned away and reached for another plate. If she kept eating off his fingers, he wouldn't be responsible for his actions. He busied himself at the pot and tipped more sauce onto the crab before reaching into the cooler for the bread. Placing a large chunk on her plate, he passed it to her, and walked around to the other side of the fire.

"It is. Nothing beats the taste of fresh cooked crab."

Jess seemed to sense he was trying to put some distance between them and she lifted up her fork and ate quietly for a few minutes. Alex leaned back against the rock to get comfortable, grateful for the fire blocking her view. He definitely needed to go out in Darwin and get back into life. But to take care of his immediate and pressing need tonight, he was going to jump back into the cold end of the pool as soon as dinner had settled, and before he turned in for the night.

"Tell me about Cockatoo Springs." Jess put her plate down on the rock and lifted the bottle of beer to her lips. Loose curls fell from the scarf she'd tied around her hair, and she lifted her other hand to push it back. Alex shook his head as the firelight caught a huge ring on her middle finger.

How many women would put jewellery on around a campfire in the outback? They were poles apart. He had nothing to worry about. That feeling of wanting to get to get to know her a little better receded a little. *Just a little.* But the other need to keep her up close and personal still strained against his jeans.

"You must know something about the resort if you have a cabin nearby."

"Yeah, I wander around the kitchens a bit."

Jess leaned back and the shawl slipped off her shoulder. Her white skin glowed with an iridescent pearliness. It had been soft and silky beneath his lips and fingers in the pool this afternoon. He itched to reach out to her and pick up where they'd left off.

Alex stood up abruptly. If he didn't get away from her, he was going to lose control. "I have to check on the truck. I want to look at the gearbox. I didn't like that noise it made when we drove in."

He knew his voice was gruff.

"I'll see you in the morning. If there's anything you need through the night, just yell. Oh, and make sure you zip up the windows, because the mozzies will stay around all night."

If he was going to be hot and uncomfortable,

she damned well could be too. He was getting more out of sorts by the minute. Why the hell did he ever offer to take her to Cockatoo Springs?

***

Blasted moody men.

They were all the same. As soon as things didn't go their way, they cracked it. One minute he was feeding her crab and gazing into her eyes like some love struck teenager, and the next minute he'd gone all rude and grumpy, and went crawling away to hide under his truck. Now she needed to find a bathroom, and the closest one was still fifty miles away at least.

I hate the outback...and camping. Give me five stars any day.

After she'd found a private spot behind the large boulders, Jess wandered over to the edge of the rock face overlooking the pool. Her feet made no sound on the sandy dirt, and she was sure Alex hadn't even noticed she was gone. The stars in the inky sky were brighter than anything she'd ever seen in the night sky, and they calmed her ill temper. She drew in a deep breath and sat on a flat rock gazing down at the water.

It was so beautiful out here. Despite the physical challenges, the vast space and the silence tugged at something deep inside her. The moon had risen while they'd sat around the fire, and now the moonlight was reflecting in the water. She really wouldn't mind spending more time in the outback and having a good look around.

She closed her eyes and imagined hiring Alex as her guide. She could find a decent vehicle—with air conditioning—and he could take her to all the beautiful places he'd talked about. If she didn't get the interview with Ricardo, the new job was toast anyway, and there was no point rushing home. The last thing she'd wanted to do was to touch her trust money, but what the hell? So what if her father thought she'd failed? She had no respect for him anyway, so she might as well make the most of it—he was loaded. She could still write her freelance articles if she didn't get the job at *Cuisine,* and travel the world.

She shook her head and pushed the thoughts away. That wasn't going to happen. She could daydream all she liked but she'd come here to get the interview and she was going to, and then the job would be hers. She was looking forward to getting to the resort and chasing him down. She'd survived the outback, how much harder was getting an appointment with the managing director.

Soft footsteps sounded behind her and her heart jumped in anticipation. She stared ahead waiting for Alex to speak to her...or touch her. Her skin prickled with anticipation and she closed her eyes. A wet nose pushed against her arm and she turned. Alex was nowhere to be seen. It was only

Bowser who'd come to check on her. She lifted the little dog up into her lap and scratched at his head.

"Just you and me, then, hey little man?"

She had some thinking to do and she needed a good night's sleep before they headed off in the morning. Putting Bowser down onto the ground, Jess turned her back on the enticing pool and the moonlight, and headed for the most interesting accommodation she'd ever stayed in.

The fire was stoked high, and disappointment filled her when she saw the campsite was deserted. She climbed into the back of the truck, determined to get Alex out of her head.

Three hours later, she gave up trying to sleep. She'd heard Alex come back into camp a while back, and the zipper of his swag had sounded, and then all was quiet. As for her accommodation, she had never been so uncomfortable in her entire life. For the umpteenth time, she climbed back up to the high side of the small space and wedged the old, tatty pillow into the space near the back door. Alex had parked the truck on an angle and each time she'd dozed off, she'd rolled down to the other side of the truck, to finish hard up against the small outboard motor.

Perspiration trickled down between her shoulder blades and she sat up trying to find some movement of cooler air in the confined space. Her long skirt was tangled around her legs. She pulled it off impatiently and threw it on top of her suitcase. Her mouth was dry, and she was so very thirsty.

That's it. I've had enough.

Taking a deep breath, she quietly unzipped the canvas. She grabbed the blanket and pillow, and backed slowly out of the truck, sighing with relief as the cool air hit her bare legs. The fire had burned down to a pile of glowing embers. Alex's swag was zipped up and there was no sign of Bowser. Jess tiptoed around to the front of the truck, quietly opened the passenger side door, and slipped the pillow and blanket onto the front seat. She'd go and look at the water for a while until she cooled down, and then she'd try sleeping in there. It had to be better than the smelly canvas tent she was sharing with the outboard motor.

Her sandals were still in the back of the truck so she walked on her toes over to the edge of the bluff, using the bright moonlight to guide her steps on the sandy ground. Bowser gave a little short bark as she tiptoed past the swag, and Alex's quiet murmur sent a shiver down her back. Settling on the same rock as before, she pulled the light shawl around her shoulders and tipped her head back to let the breeze cool her face. She was wide awake now and the thought of trying to sleep in the front of the truck didn't appeal at all. A soon as they got to the resort, she could play catch up on her sleep…as well as hair treatments, showers, and manicures. Quiet footsteps sounded behind her and her skin tingled with anticipation.

Please.

"Are you okay?"

"Yes, just hot…and the accommodation is slightly smelly."

He cleared his throat and she looked up to a smile.

"I should have offered you the swag, but—"

"But what?"

"Nothing."

He turned away from her, ran his hand through his hair, and stared out across the water. His jeans were unbuttoned and hung low on his waist, his strong, bare shoulders outlined by the moonlight. He must have sensed her gaze and he turned slowly back to her. The blood pounded through Jess's veins and she waited, the electricity between them almost crackling in the air.

She jumped as a huge white flash lit up the sky. "Holy hell! What was that?"

"You're in for a treat. There's a dry storm brewing."

"How do you know it's a dry storm and it won't rain?" All she could think of was being stranded here for another night in that smelly space. She couldn't decide if that would be a good or a bad outcome.

"It will rain over on the coast. We'll just get to see the spectacular light show from up here."

Alex held his hand out to her and she looked up at him. "What?"

"Come on. We'll go down to the pool for a swim. It'll be cooler and the mozzies will stay away. We'll still get a good view of the storm from down there."

Jess took his hand and tucked the shawl around her shoulders, conscious of her bare legs. He led her down the rocky incline to the water. He gripped her hand without speaking, and tension hummed through her body. She let go of his hand when they reached the bottom of the waterfall and dropped her shawl to the ground. Slipping into the warm water, she floated on her back and watched the flashes in the sky that were becoming more frequent. A soft splash at the far end of the pool told her Alex was in the water with her. The water rippled around her and a sleek, black head broke the surface beside her. Alex turned to his back and floated next to her.

"Where's Bowser?" she asked.

"In the truck. I put him in there so he wouldn't chew my swag up."

Jess laughed.

"Yes, I've seen what he did to my bed."

They didn't speak for a few moments and floated together on top of the water watching the blue, pink, and dark green flashes filling the sky as the storm broke over on the coast.

"Amazing," Jess whispered. "Thank you so much for bringing me out here."

"To the pool?"

"No, out here." She lowered her feet to the sandy bottom and lifted her arm in a sweeping gesture. "Out here to all this. It is amazing. You've converted me to the outback, Alex."

"It is pretty special. I can't imagine being anywhere else."

"In fact, I've pretty much decided to stick around a while longer."

"What do you mean stick around?" Even in the moonlight, Jess could see his eyes narrow.

"After I get the interview, I've might extend my holiday. If there's room, I'll stay at Cockatoo Springs and take some of the tours."

She looked at him and an unfamiliar shyness filled her. "Ah…how would you feel about showing me around a bit more if I did stay for a bit longer?"

"Do you know how expensive it is out here?" Alex put his hands on her shoulders, and her heart took off as the blood zinged around her body. "I thought you needed to keep your job. That's why you had to get this interview."

She shot him a glance and his brow was wrinkled in a frown. "Look if it bothers you that much to spend any more time with me, I'll just do my own thing. Forget I ever mentioned it."

"It doesn't bother me." His fingers pressed into her shoulders. "Well, it does in one way."

"What way?"

Alex groaned and pulled her close, and heat rushed through her.

"This way." He grabbed her hair in his hands and tipped her head back, his mouth crushing hers. Jess lifted her legs and wrapped them around his waist, the slickness of his bare skin burning hers even in the cool water. She stroked his back, her fingers sliding over his wet skin, and his muscles bunched beneath her hands. He raised his head and looked at her, the moonlight shadowing his rugged face. Jess leaned forward and nibbled at his bottom lip, running her fingers through the long wet hair that clung to his neck

"Your place or mine?" she murmured against his mouth.

"Mine" he said with a quiet laugh. "I thing Bowser's in yours now."

***

Alex followed Jess up the hill, unable to keep his hands away from her. He bent and put his arms beneath her knees, sweeping her into his arms and strode the short distance to the swag. The heat between them pushed all thoughts of anything but the feel of her from his mind.

"Boy scout?" she whispered against his lips and

sanity returned for a brief moment. Alex stood her gently on the ground and reached down to unzip the swag.

"Get in there and wait for me, woman." His heart rate picked up even more as she ran a finger down his chest and reached up to kiss him.

"Don't be long." Even her voice was temptation.

Jess bent and climbed into the swag, and the sight of her long legs disappearing into the small tent was enough to make Alex pick up the pace as he strode across to his truck.

"Stay." Bowser turned his back and curled back up on the floor as Alex scrabbled on the floor until he found the small box he'd thrown through the window earlier. A moment later, he dropped down and crawled into the swag where Jess was waiting for him. Alex caught his breath—she was every bit as beautiful as he'd imagined.

Jess drew a breath as he kneeled beside her. He placed his hands on each side of her face and took her mouth in a slow gentle kiss, and then lay down beside her. She lifted her head, feathering kisses along his jaw.

"Alex?" Her voice was soft and wanting.

"What's the matter?"

"Not fair," she whispered against his lips.

"What's not fair?" He lifted his head and looked down at her.

"You've got the five star room."

"Okay, caught out," he said. "I admit it. I was trying to teach you a lesson."

"What sort of lesson?"

"A lesson about the danger of taking lifts with strangers in the outback." He laughed. "But it sort of backfired on me, didn't it?"

She shot a grin up at him. "I think it turned out pretty well…for both of us. I can only see one problem."

"What's that?" He dropped another kiss on her nose. "It's a long way to the en suite."

She held out her arms and he took up where he left off when she'd interrupted him.

Chapter Eleven

Jess squeezed the water from her hair and let it run down her neck. The temperature of the pool was cooler this morning because the sun hadn't reached its peak yet. Alex wanted to get an early start.

They'd had little sleep through the night, and he was keen to get on the road before it rained. The sky was dark and heavy, very different from the starry clear sky that had been above them when they went down for another swim in the middle of the night. They'd dived and frolicked, unable to keep their hands off each other. Their play was interrupted by trailing fingers and lingering kisses at regular intervals.

When they dried off and returned to the swag, Jess dropped into a deep sleep until Alex woke her at sunrise, pointing to the ominous sky, and she'd hurried down the hill for a quick wash. If she was turning up at a luxury world-class resort, she wanted to look the part. Or at least somewhat clean.

She climbed the rocky slope and Alex's deep voice reached her. He beckoned her over as he spoke on the phone.

"Thanks, mate. Yeah, it's a shame. I'll tell her and get back to you to book the helicopter seat."

He reached over and put the phone back inside the truck, a frown on his face. "Sorry, Jess. Bad news."

"For me or you?"

"I suppose it depends which way you look at it." Alex put his arms loosely around her waist and held her gaze. "No room at the inn, as they say."

"Oh no, it's full?"

"Yes. My mate, Mitch, checked for me. So, what now?"

"Do you want me to get them to book the helicopter to Darwin for you?"

Disappointment pierced Jess's chest. Until a minute ago, Alex had been friendly and playful, even after he took the call. Something had changed his mood instantly, and she had no idea what she'd done.

"I still want to try and get my interview." She folded her arms across her chest and stuck her chin out. "I'm not going to spend two days crossing the outback and then just hop into a helicopter and go home. It would have all been for nothing."

Alex grabbed her shoulders and stared down at her. "All of it, Jess? All for nothing?" He dropped his head and took her mouth in a hard kiss. She stepped back and touched her fingers to her lips.

"No, some of it was good. Wonderful, in

fact." When he turned away without commenting, she followed him, wanting to lash out. She was sick of men and their ability to hurt her. At least with Harrison she'd known he was after her money. Alex knew nothing—or very little—about the real Jess and still he turned away from her. Tears stung the backs of her eyes and she couldn't help the feeling that it was all coming to an end. "Yes, the scenery was magnificent and the swimming hole was fun. Yesterday, you offered me a room at your place. Does that offer still stand, or now that you've had your fun with the easy Yank, have you changed your mind?"

"Jess, don't talk like that." He strode over to the fire and began to pack up, and she knew he didn't want to be near her. "Don't put yourself down."

"Well, does the room offer still stand?" Her voice sounded as though she was begging and she hated it. "I'd love to stay with you while I chase up Ricardo. And my great organisational skills have kicked in yet again and now there's no room at the resort, so can I stay with you or not?"

Alex ran his hand through his hair and absentmindedly dug in his pocket for a piece of string. He held her gaze while he tied his hair back. His cheeks were covered with dark stubble and his expression was grim. If she hadn't known better, she would have found him intimidating, but she knew he was a good person. He'd looked out for her throughout the trip, and it was only this morning that he'd changed back into the gruff fisherman.

Something was bothering him.

"Did you get some bad news on the telephone? Oh well, it's none of my business." She turned away and gathered up her things and looked down at her dirty clothes. "Besides, they probably wouldn't have given me a room anyway looking like a stray from the outback."

Warm hands descended on her shoulders, and she held his gaze.

"I offered a room to you and I am a man of my word." Alex tugged gently on her arm, and Jess turned around to face him. "If you want to stay, my offer still stands."

He held her gaze and she tried not to react as she looked up into his deep blue eyes, wanting to ignore the warm shivers that were igniting a fire low in her belly.

"I don't want to see you disappointed when you don't get your interview," he said. "I like you, Jess. I like you a little too much for my own peace of mind, and I'd hate to see you hurt."

"That's a strange term to use, Alex. Disappointed maybe, but not hurt."

He leaned down and brushed a much gentler kiss across her lips. "Come on, I want to beat this rain."

Quietly she helped him pack up the truck and throw sand on the glowing embers of the fire. As Jess walked to the truck and opened the door, she looked around. She would always hold this campsite in the middle of the outback close to her heart.

***

When Jess had chewed her lip and looked up at him with those wide green eyes, remorse had spiked Alex's chest. Unfamiliar warmth that had nothing to do with sex stole over him, and he knew he didn't want to hurt this woman. There was only one way this could end if she found out who he was. She'd assume he'd been lying to her about everything and slaked his sexual need with the 'easy Yank' as she'd called herself. Someone had obviously done a number on her. Underneath her confidence, he could see how sensitive she was, and easy to hurt.

Shit. He was going to be so bloody careful when they reached Cockatoo Springs. As well as not wanting to reveal who he was to a freelance journalist, he didn't want to hurt her either.

He turned the truck onto the road and glanced across at Jess. Bowser was curled up on her lap, and she was staring thoughtfully out the window.

Easy Yank. Nothing could be further from the truth, and he felt guilty that she thought that. He wanted her on that helicopter and out of here before she could mess up his life and get herself hurt in the process. He'd been more than content, happy with the way things were, before she'd arrived on the scene.

Mitch had been taken aback when he'd told him he was bringing in a guest, and more so when he'd asked him to say there were no rooms available. In reality, the resort was half-empty, but he didn't want her anywhere near it, snooping around without him nearby. It would get busier in a couple of days when Clay ran his first course and the international chefs arrived on the helicopter from Darwin If she still insisted on staying with him, he would have to keep her close by. And that was going to be hard because the CEO of the luxury travel company was there for their meeting. Mitch said he'd flown in early, and if he didn't see him straight away, the deal was at risk. It was the last big deal he had to finalise before his contract came to an end, so he'd have to book Jess on a tour tomorrow if she stayed, while he got himself cleaned up and into a business meeting.

And my family is about to hit the resort too. Alex ran his hand through his hair.

"Worried?"

"Huh?"

"You look worried," she said. "Are you worried about the rain coming?"

"No, we'll be fine. Mitch said it's clear over

on the coast." He straightened his shoulders and smiled at her. "It's only about a two-hour drive from here. I'll bet you're wishing you took the helicopter in? The flight from Darwin only takes twenty minutes."

"I've seen the true outback." She lifted her hands and her brow wrinkled in a frown. "But a manicure will be nice."

"So you're going to stay for a day or so?"

She glanced across at him from beneath her lashes. "More if the mood takes me. It all depends on what happens when we get there."

Shit. He would have to put a plan in place fast. He wasn't used to this sort of double dealing. Using Alessandro Ricardo for the business promotion had never been a problem before. Mitch handled the staff and he'd always had the business meetings with clients in Darwin. Because of the isolation of the resort the mostly backpacker staff changed over frequently, and they rarely stayed more than a few months. Those who knew him, knew him as simply, Alex the fisherman. But he had a feeling his life was about to get very complicated.

Chapter Twelve

Alex held the door open and gestured for her to enter the small cabin. Jess had been expecting a fishing cabin like the one at Daly River where he'd picked up the boat, but this cabin beside the resort was quite luxurious.

"Is this yours?" She turned to him curiously as he followed her inside.

"Ah…sort of." He bent down and picked up Bowser, carried him across to the sink in the small utility room, and turned the tap on to fill the tub. "I…er… rent it from the resort and use it as a base most if the time I'm up here." Alex looked away and busied himself with Bowser, lifting him into the tub, and sponging the red dust of his coat. "Let me clean up this little guy and then I'll show you around."

Jess wandered across to the window past a white leather sofa. Soft *flokati* rugs were scattered across the polished timber floor. The whole place screamed money, and she could see why Bowser was having a wash before he was allowed inside.

A water sprinkler spun lazily in the early afternoon sun throwing rainbows across the lush grass at the front of the cabin. Across the road, a gleaming expanse of white sand shimmered in the midday sun, and in the far distance a couple strolled along the beach hand in hand.

Alex walked across to the window, towelling the dog with a large white cloth.

"So, we're close to the resort?" she asked.

"Yes." He put the dog down and Bowser's claws tapped on the timber floor as he ran across to Jess and put his paws up on her knees.

Alex stood close, and she could feel the heat the heat of his body. She closed her eyes, fighting the need to lean into him.

"Yes, it's just through that high hedge over there. See that wall? There's a gate a short way along." He moved away and Jess opened her eyes as he opened a door leading out to the small front balcony. She followed him and he pointed to the north when she heard a helicopter.

"There's the early afternoon helicopter. It comes in twice a day. Few people come here by road. The boat comes in twice a week and brings a lot of the supplies in." He leaned back on the timber railing and stared at her intently. "Do you want me to see if I can get you onto the helicopter tomorrow morning?"

Jess clenched her jaw and gripped the railing. "Alex, just come straight to the point." She didn't look at him and kept her eyes on the dark blue helicopter that was swooping low over the beach. "I appreciate that you got me here, but if you don't want me to stay here, just come out and say it. I told you I didn't come all this way to get here and give up."

Alex didn't speak until the helicopter disappeared, and the only sound was the wind rustling the palm trees on the sandy beach in front of them. He put his hand over hers on the railing, and she held her breath waiting for his reply.

"I just don't want you disappointed." He gazed out to the water. "It's going to be boring for you. You won't be able to go to the resort. They…I mean… Mitch...is really strict about that. The facilities are only for guests." He slapped his free hand on his hip and turned to her. "I know what I can try for you. I will ask Mitch if you can go on one of the tours while you are here. There's probably a bush tucker tour tomorrow. What do you reckon?"

"What do I reckon?" She grinned at him, mimicking his Australian drawl. "I reckon that sounds just the sort of thing that would help me find out a bit more about Ricardo's chef school."

Hope filled her. Maybe she could go on the bush tucker tour, get to spend more time with Alex, and get material for her article at the same time.

"As long as I have a bed." Heat filled her cheeks as she thought of sharing a real bed with him. "I'll do the tour and stay a couple of days."

She looked at him as determination filled her. "I'm not sure about what to do yet. I might check out the restaurant before I go looking for Ricardo. If you've any friends in the kitchen, perhaps you could ask if there are any kitchen hands needed? I could do some hands-on research."

"Okay." He lifted his hand from hers. "Come on. I'll show you your room and get your bags out of the truck. While you get yourself settled, I'll see Mitch about…the fish. So, I'll ask around for you."

Alex showed her a small bedroom off the living room and pointed out the adjacent bathroom before he went to the truck and brought her bags to the back porch. He set them down and went into the utility room, and came back out with a handful of cloths.

"Sorry. It's got a bit dusty, and I think the oil from the outboard has leaked into one of your bags. There's a washing machine in the cupboard if you want to wash anything while I'm gone."

"Thanks." Jess took the cloths from him and began to wipe the red dust from her large suitcase.

"Make yourself at home." Alex reached around the doorway and flicked a switch.
"That'll cool the place down a bit for you." He walked over to the truck and opened the door. "There's coffee in here, but no food. I'll be gone a while, but I'll sort dinner out. I'll leave the cooler

here in case you get hungry, and Jess, be careful. Don't go wandering around. The resort is fenced in, but this cabin is out in the open, and there could be salties around."

"Great," she muttered to herself as the truck drove off. "Don't worry. I won't be going anywhere."

She'd been stuck with him in a pickup for the last forty-eight hours. What was one more day stuck in his cabin?

###

Jess unpacked and rinsed the red dirt from her clothes, putting anything that wasn't made of silk in the small clothes drier. Alex had her so spooked about crocodiles slithering through the garden she wasn't brave enough to go to the small clothesline outside on the grass, so she draped her silk shirts and wraps over the living room furniture. She took a quick shower in the bathroom, surprised at the luxury of Italian tiles in a worker's cabin.

Wandering into the bedroom where Alex had put her other bags, Jess hitched up the towel tied around her chest. It was a large white bath towel monogrammed with the letters 'CS'—the resort obviously looked after this cabin. Alex said he'd be a while, and she was waiting for her things to dry. Jess reached up and twirled her wet hair into a knot and dug into her bag for a clip, and her fingers brushed against her phone.

"Shit, Monica."

Grabbing it, she turned it on and sighed with relief when five high bars indicated full service. She hadn't given Monica a thought all day, and her friend was probably panicking wondering what the hell had happened to her.

Yep, eight missed calls.

Every hour, on the hour, until a couple of hours ago.

Jess pressed the return call button, and held her wet hair back with one hand waiting for the greeting she knew would come.

"Jessica Trent!"

She held the phone away from her ear as the usual high-pitched squeal was amplified through the phone. She let Monica speak for a full minute before she interrupted.

"Calm down, Mon. I'm okay."

"Where the hell have you been? Is there no phone service in the outback? That had better be the case, Jessica, because I am fit to kill you. Even Gareth was worried when you didn't call."

"I'm okay. I've just arrived at the Cockatoo Springs…sort of."

"Where have you been? Did you get the interview yet? What do you mean sort of?"

"No, no interview yet. I had a bit of a detour. I'll tell you all about it when I get home."

"So what's the deal with Ricardo? Can you

get an appointment with him?"

Jess sighed. "I'll tell you all about it when I come home. I'm back in civilisation now. I'll email if I have any news and let you know when I'm flying out. I don't even know if Ricardo is here, he is such a recluse."

"He *is* there," Monica said.

Jess dropped her wet hair and sat forward on the edge of the bed. It fell to her shoulder and cool water trickled down between her breasts and she took a quick breath as Monica continued.

"There's a big deal going down. Gareth was reading the *Wall Street Journal* to me this morning and commented on how great your timing was."

"What sort of deal?"

"Larry Bartholomew, *your* boss, is over there with one of his other companies, Worldwide Luxury Tours. Apparently, he's at Cockatoo Springs negotiating with Ricardo as we speak."

Jess jumped up and did a happy dance, punching the air as Monica continued. "All you have to do is wander around the resort until you bump into him, and voila, one look at Jess Trent, the beautiful journalist and you will have no trouble getting Ricardo to talk to you."

Ricardo was here. First problem solved. But getting him to talk to her was going to be a bit harder than what Monica thought. She was going to have to approach this very carefully, especially with

Larry in the picture.

"It's going to be a little bit tougher than that, I think. I can't believe Larry's over here. And I can't just wander around, I'm not even—" Jess cut off her words so she didn't have to explain it all to Monica and flopped back down on the bed. She dropped her head into one hand.

Wander around the resort? How the hell was she going to do that?

"Mon, do me a favour?"

"What?" Monica's voice was suspicious. "I know your favours."

"Oh, for goodness' sake. All I want is the phone number for Cockatoo Springs."

"Why? Just look at the stuff in your room. They always have it all over the pens and books next to the bed."

Jessica took a deep breath. "Sweets, just look up the number for me and I'll explain when I get back."

"Okay, give me one minute. I'll Google it."

Opening the sliding glass door to the small veranda off her room, Jess stood looking across at the high brick wall covered with tropical vines as Monica looked for the number. So close…

"Here it is."

She hurried back inside and grabbed a pen and wrote the number on the back of her business card.

"You're a lifesaver. I'll email you as soon as I get my computer hooked up to the Wi Fi."

"Jess, what's happening over there? I know when you're up to something. Just keep safe, okay?"

"Don't stress. I'm having a fabulous break, and I've got lots to tell you." She ended the call and threw her phone onto the bed before hurrying into the bathroom to dry her hair and put some make-up on. If all went to plan, she was going to brave the crocodiles, get over to the resort, and get her interview after all.

Chapter Thirteen

"Bloody hell, Alex." Mitch, his assistant manager and long-time friend slapped a hand to his forehead and shook his head. "Look at you. The most important business meeting you've had all year and you look like the wild man of Borneo."

"Yeah, I know, I know. I have to get a haircut and clean up."

"Have a shower, find a suit, and I'll send one of the girls from the beauty salon over to the villa to give you a haircut."

"No. I'm over in the cabin…and you can't send anyone over there."

"Has this got something to do with that phone call about not having any empty rooms?"

"Yeah, we have—or I have— a problem. I have a journalist over there determined to interview Ricardo."

"And you found her in the middle of the outback?" Mitch shook his head and held his hands up, an incredulous expression on his face. "No, don't explain, we haven't got time. Bartholomew was furious when you weren't here this morning."

"Stuff him, that's his problem." Alex

walked around the desk and sat in the chair. "I'll see him when I'm ready. He needs us more than we need him, from what I've been reading. He can wait."

"Sometimes I think I worry more about the success of this place more than you do. You're never really happy unless you are out in the wilds." Mitch sat on the chair opposite Alex and ran his hand through his short-cropped hair.

"I've only got to worry about it till next week. Contract's up and I'm out of here."

"So you've paid your dues?" Mitch said quietly. He was the only one Alex had confided in, and it had helped Mitch respect his request to stay private.

"Yes, the Emily Young School of Bush Tucker has made its mark in the food world and I can move on."

"So, tell me about this journalist? How did you hook up with her?"

"She's beautiful, brave, and I think…no, I know, I'm in trouble here, mate." He stared past Mitch and didn't speak for a moment. When he looked back at his manager, he was the subject of a very intense gaze. "I can't get her out of my head. For the first time in a long time, I've let a woman get under my skin."

"So, what's the problem? Tell her who you are, make her sign a confidentiality agreement, and a no-reveal clause of your identity in her newspaper. Move her into the villa, have a fling, and send her on her way."

"She doesn't work for a newspaper. She works for Larry Bartholomew's media company."

"That's a bit suss. Do you think he sent her? Was she scoping you out?"

"No, she doesn't know I'm Alessandro."

"Are you sure? It seems a bit coincidental she's over here the same time as her boss. Does it really matter to you that she doesn't find out who you are?"

Alex shrugged. "When I came up here after Emily died, I promised her family I'd get the place started. You saw how messed up I was. It suited me then, and it suits me now to finish up when the contracted time is up. I don't want my photos plastered over a magazine and all my life laid out for public consumption. Alessandro Ricardo can disappear gracefully." He stood and wandered over to the wall and looked at the awards of recognition they'd received over the years. "You've done a great job as the front man, Mitch, and I've appreciated being able to stay behind the scenes. It was such a stupid idea, the idea of having a mysterious owner, although it did get us a lot of international press. I'm ready to move on."

Mitch followed him over and clapped him on the shoulder. "Maybe it's time to say it is Alex

Richards running the show?"

Alex looked out across the resort, past the high brick fence in the direction of the cabin. "No, there's no need now. I'll get Jess in the kitchen. She can get some information for her article, and then we'll go our separate ways. I don't need any more complications in my life. I'm keeping it simple."

###

Before he went back to the kitchens to meet the new chef, Alex made a quick detour to his own large villa at the beach side of the resort. He pulled out his suit and hung it in on the door to air for his meeting tomorrow. Glancing around the walls at the photographs of his family, he smiled. They'd all descend on Cockatoo Springs for his birthday next weekend, and he was looking forward to seeing them. Which reminded him, he'd forgotten to organise to keep her busy tomorrow. He picked up the phone and dialled Mitch's extension.

"I forgot to ask you. Is there a bush tucker tour tomorrow?"

"Yeah, leaves at seven thirty."

"Can you book Jessica Trent on it for me?"

"Will do. How do you want to handle it? Will you take her to the bus or get her collected at the cabin?"

"Yes, at the cabin. Tell Terence to collect her there. I don't want her wandering around just yet."

Next stop was the kitchens, and Alex pulled up and went around to the back of the truck and unzipped the canvas at the back of the pickup. He took a step back as the combined smells of fish, gas, and dog hit him full on. Stepping forward, he reached back in to lift out the cooler full of mud crabs and he grinned.

No wonder Jess had ended up in my swag. Maybe it hadn't been my rugged sex appeal after all

He pushed open the door to the air-conditioned kitchen and placed the cooler on the stainless-steel bench.

"Anyone around?" He wandered into the restaurant, pausing when he saw the chefs, the sous-chefs, and the kitchen hands sitting at the tables taking notes. An unfamiliar man in chef trousers and a patterned bandanna tying his black, curly hair back, stepped over with his hand outstretched.

"You must be Alessandro. Mitch said you'd be bringing the crabs."

He ushered the new chef back out to the kitchen, away from the curious looks of the staff, before he held his hand out to him "Clay, great to meet you."

"Likewise. Thanks for the barramundi. It arrived last night and we're already planning a feast tonight. Quite a few guests flew in today, and we've got some food journalists in too."

Alex groaned.

"Jeez, they must be stalking me," he muttered, wondering how to handle it. His life had become way too complicated over the past two days.

Take me back to the scrub and the fish.

Clay tipped his head to the side with a frown. "Problem? How do you want me to handle them? Interviews or not?"

"No. Just feed them and if they ask any questions, tell them he will be putting out a press release in a day or so."

"Alessandro? Sorry, I thought you were Alessandro."

Alex gave a wry laugh. "Long story, mate. I'll fill you in over a welcoming beer later. Anyway—" He reached out and shook Clay's hand again. "Great to have you on board." He went to the large cool room and opened the door. Reaching in, he pulled out a bottle of chilled white wine before turning back to the chef.

"A favour, mate? I've got a friend staying who'd like to see how the place works. Could you do with another kitchen hand for a few days?"

"If she's got no food handling certificate, she'll be on wash up duty. That okay?"

"That's fine. Her name's Jess and I'm just Alex when you talk about me, if you do, Okay? No mention of Alessandro."

Clay grinned at him. "Whatever you say,

you're the boss."

Alex headed for the door, picking the empty cooler up on the way. "Can you get one of the staff to bring two meals over to my cabin? Make sure you tell them I'm in the cabin, not the villa."

Clay gave him a wave. "No problem."

Chapter Fourteen

Jess put her mobile back into her bag and stared out the window, confusion filling her mind. She'd dialled the number Monica gave her for Cockatoo Springs, the same resort Alex had told her only today was full. The reservations clerk had just informed her rooms were available now.

Now, as in today. Right now.

Of course she hadn't told him she was right next door. Why would Alex have said there were no rooms? A warm feeling filled her chest, but it was quickly followed by uncertainty.

If he'd been so keen to have her stay, he could have just asked her, there was no need for game playing. Anyway, he'd seemed more enthusiastic about her getting on the helicopter, and going home than anything else. Maybe he had a girlfriend…or a wife, God forbid, here on the resort. But she shook her head. If that were true he wouldn't have installed her into his cabin.

Would he?

Jess's heart gave a crazy leap when Bowser yapped and jumped up. His ears pricked and his little head cocked to the side. The now familiar sound of Alex's pickup truck roared in through the screened door where the dog stood whimpering. She stood and smoothed her hand over her hair as she walked across to greet him, her silk skirt swishing softly against her bare legs, her bracelets jangling on her wrist. A shower, clean clothes, and access to the world via her telephone had restored her equilibrium, and now she was going to put on the performance of her life to hide the confusion filling her. Closing her eyes, she waited for the door to open to see how he would greet her. Was he hoping she might have gone, or would he be pleased to see her?

The door squeaked and then all was quiet until a low wolf whistle came from across the room. Her heart thudding, she turned and met Alex's gaze. His eyes were hooded and he looked at her for a long moment before speaking.

"What have you done with my Jess?"

"Your Jess?" Her own low throaty voice surprised her.

"Yeah, my Jess of the Outback." His face lit up in a wide grin. "You know, the one with the string in her hair and the dirty clothes?"

"Sorry, can't help you there. Haven't seen her." She smoothed down her brightly patterned silk skirt with a shaking hand. Alex walked over to her, his bare feet quiet on the timber floor, and took her hand in his. He picked it up and examined the short-clipped fingernails, free of red nail polish.

"They're her hands," he said softly as he lifted her hand to his lips, turned it, and kissed her open palm.

She swayed toward him, but he gently grasped her wrist and held her away before he dipped his head and lightly brushed her mouth with his lips.

"Let me take a quick shower and then I'll tell you my news."

"News? Have you talked to Ricardo?"

"Patience, my dear." He dropped her arm and went back outside, returning with a bottle of wine. "Pour the wine. I'll be quick and then I'll tell you."

Jess muttered to herself as she opened the wine and searched through the cupboards for some glasses. The kitchen was bare, and the room was more like a hotel room, with only essentials.

Opening the last door, she cheered to herself as she found the glasses. She tried to block the picture of the water droplets on Alex's muscled chest. She poured her wine, and put the bottle and the other glass in the refrigerator, next to the jug of water, which was the only other thing in there.

Maybe he'll take me over to the restaurant for dinner? Maybe I'll get to see Cockatoo Springs tonight?

Moving across to the window, she looked

out at the ocean, flat and silver in the soft moonlight. The sun had set just before Alex had come back and the night in the outback seemed to descend with no dusk. She leaned her forehead on the cool glass and tried to focus. Hopefully, he'd heard Ricardo was there too and spoken to him already, singing the praises of the journalist who wanted to interview him.

Ha, and pigs might fly too.

The bathroom door closed and the smell of fresh soap drifted across to her. The fridge door opened and the clink of the wine bottle clicking on the glass filled the quiet room. Outside, it was silent, and the bright lights of the resort next door lit up the night. Alex came out of the kitchen holding his wine glass, pausing in the doorway where he leaned on the frame and sipped his wine, looking at her.

A loose white shirt hung over a pair of knee length chinos. Jess turned slowly, and desire shot straight through her.

"Welcome to Cockatoo Springs."

"Thank you." She walked over and clinked her glass against his. He reached up and held her hand.

"You look beautiful, Jess. I should have taken you out tonight."

"To the resort?" she asked hopefully. "Maybe we could we go there for dinner? My treat to thank you for the ride here."

Alex led her over to the leather sofa and sat down, pulling her next to him. She looked at his tanned legs brushing against her pale calves. He followed her gaze and lifted her legs up across his lap, and a shiver ran along her back when he trailed his fingers along her toes.

"No need to thank me. Dinner is being delivered to the cabin. We have the whole night to ourselves."

A curl of anticipation wound its way through her body.

"I can think of better ways to spend the night than sitting at some restaurant." His voice was low, and he didn't take his eyes from hers. "Not a mosquito or a crocodile to disturb us."

"Or a pig?" She laughed, and it dispelled the sexual tension gripping her.

His laugh was deep and sexy. "You really did cope with the outback very well for a first timer."

"I will never forget the sight of you up that tree in your underwear."

"Aw, come on, Jess, you're supposed to remember me saving you. I'm the outback hero, remember?"

"That is how I'll remember you when I go back to New York. A real Crocodile Dundee," she said softly. "Now tell me what's happening. Did you find out if there is a tour tomorrow?"

"Yep. After I dropped the crabs off, I went over to the office. You're booked on the tour that leaves at seven thirty in the morning. They'll pick you up here at the cabin, and they'll take you out to the grasslands in a small four-wheel drive bus and show you how to collect all sorts of bush tucker. One of the chefs goes on the trip and they cook damper for morning tea and flavour it with the bush tucker you collect."

"Damper?"

"A loaf of bread baked in the fire."

"Sounds great." She lifted her wine glass to her lips. "And did you find out about Ricardo?"

Alex shook his head slowly and frowned. "Sorry, Jess. He's not there at the moment."

"Oh." Disappointment shot through her. Damn him. If Monica was right, Alex was lying to her. She'd said Ricardo was here for a meeting with Larry. And that was another problem.

Even though she would try to meet Ricardo and get that interview, she'd keep a low profile if Larry were around. As well as being her boss, he was one of her father's *nouvelle riche* buddies. She was going to have to play it very carefully if he *was* here with Ricardo. She didn't want him to know she was after the interview until the article was in the bag, and the less her father knew about her whereabouts, and what she was doing, suited her just fine. But why was Alex so damned determined she had to forget about this interview?

She looked up and his gaze was fixed on her, and she could have sworn there was a flush on his cheeks. "Well, I guess I'll just have to use the bush tucker trip for information and then see if I can chase him up at his conference."

"I've got more good news for you."

She tipped her head to the side. Alex reached up and lifted her hand to his mouth.

"The day after your bush tucker tour, you've got a start as a kitchen hand washing dishes in the school kitchen. That should give you an insight into how the school works. You can stay here in my cabin for a few days. I'll take you over to meet the chef tomorrow."

Jess squealed and launched herself at him. "That is wonderful. Thank you so much."

"Clay, the chef, has got you on wash up duty. You'll soon get sick of that." He slid his hand around the back of her neck, and anticipation curled in her stomach. "More wine?"

She nodded, and Alex lifted his hand away. Jess put her head back on the soft leather of the sofa as he went to refill her glass. Three stairs led up to a low mezzanine level where the master bedroom was located. A wide timber railing ran along the edge of the room and small glass candleholders with tea candles inside were placed at small intervals. It really was a romantic little cabin. Things were looking up—a bush tucker tour, and an in into the kitchen, and a night in Alex's cabin. She might get this article written yet.

Alex came back out with the wine bottle, and she held her glass up for a refill.

"I have to go out really early tomorrow. I have some things to organise before I return to Daly River late next week." He put the bottle on the floor next to the sofa, reached over, and brought her legs back up onto his lap.

"So, you spend a bit of time in this cabin?"

"On and off."

"Would you call it home or do you live somewhere else?"

"What's with the twenty questions, Jess? I'm a pretty boring bloke."

"Oh, I don't know. I was thinking about writing that other article with you as the outback hero. If I can't have Ricardo, I can write about you. You could take your shirt off and lean across the front of your pickup or wrestle a crocodile or something." She reached over and ran her hand down his chest.

Alex choked on his wine and coughed. He put his glass on the floor next to the bottle and put his hand over his mouth. Jess patted him on the back as his face went red and his eyes watered as he shook his head.

"I don't think that would sell many magazines or help you keep your job. I thought this was a do or die interview to save your job?"

Jess trailed her fingers up his cheek and wiped the dampness beneath his eye with her thumb. "If it doesn't work out, I'll keep writing till I get a job at another magazine." She tipped her head to the side. "Outback dude chases pig on a hunting magazine cover maybe. Oh, how I wish I'd taken a photo."

He pursed his lips and frowned, and she couldn't hold her laughter back.

"Oh Alex, for such a tough guy, you are so easy to tease."

With a low growl, he grabbed her hand and tugged her so her bottom slid up into his lap. "I'll show you how to tease, woman."

Before she could reply, his lips descended on hers in a hard kiss and Jess forgot all about pigs, magazine articles, and jobs.

Jess closed her eyes as his lips caressed hers

"You confuse me, Alex," she whispered. He kept his gaze on her and smiled a slow lazy smile as he held her close. She pushed all of her worries out of her mind.

Just them. She could worry later.

"I love touching you. Your skin is like silk." His fingers lingered on her shoulders.

She slid off him and soon she was lying

beneath him, smoothing her hands over his back beneath his shirt. Impatiently he shrugged it off but stilled as there was a loud knock at the door.

"Alex? Are you in there?"

"Alex?" There was a loud knock on the door. "Are you there?"

Alex pulled his shirt back on "You might like to sit up. Our dinner has arrived," he whispered. "Coming!" he shouted to the person at the door.

Jess sat up on the sofa hastily rearranging her clothing. She ran her hands through her hair, which she knew would be in a cloud of disarray.

"Come in, Mitch." Alex's voice was strained, and Jess looked across to the door curious to see who it was.

"I was in the kitchen when they asked one of the kitchen hands to bring your dinner over." The tall blond-haired man placed a tray on the dining room table and glanced across at Jess with a quick smile. "I was walking over here so I said I'd take it over."

He sauntered across the room and smiled at her.

"Hi, I'm Mitch… a mate of this big lug here. I hope he's been looking after you. Shame we couldn't give you a room."

"Yes, it was a shame," she said watching them. "I was so looking forward to staying at Cockatoo Springs, but silly me, I forgot to book and then you were all full up!"

Satisfaction filled her as she intercepted a look between the two men. There were rooms available. The lie had been deliberate and they both knew it, but she wasn't going to let on that she'd woken up to whatever it was they were doing.

"Did you say you walked over?"

"Yes," Mitch said and Alex frowned. "It's a lovely night."

"What about the crocodiles?"

"Crocodiles?" He almost gulped as he shot a look at Alex. "What about them?"

"I thought it was unsafe to roam around because of the salties."

"Oh yes. I just know where to walk," Mitch said hurriedly backing away toward the door.

She narrowed her eyes as he smiled at her.

"Anyway, nice to meet you, Jess." He turned to Alex who was standing by the door tight-lipped.

"Alex, have you got a minute? I want to talk about the…fish." Mitch walked to the door, and after he and Alex had gone outside Jess moved across to the table. Delicious aromas were coming from beneath the covered tray and she lifted the lid as her temper built.

***

Alex got rid of Mitch as quickly as he could.

"Watch out for the salties on your way back," he called out. Mitch turned and gave him a thumbs up.

He closed the door behind him and walked in.

Whoa.

She was looking at him, and it wasn't pretty. Walking up to him with a damn you-look on her face, she poked a finger in his chest, and he took a step back. "So, what was that all about?"

"What?" He widened his eyes and tried to look innocent.

"He came to see you about the fish and braved the crocodiles, did he? What brave friends you have. You're *all* outback heroes. You tell me, why are you so determined to keep me here in your cabin and away from the resort? So much that you lied about it and cooked up some scheme with your friend."

Before he could answer, Jess pulled a chair out and sat down and put her elbows on the table, her fingers clenched in front of her chin. "Don't bother answering. I'll figure it out. Now I'm going to eat and then I'm going to bed. Alone."

The meal was silent. Alex dug deep for conversation to break the ice, but every time he opened his mouth to speak, Jess stared him down. After they'd finished the crab soup, he pushed his plate away. "What's really eating you, Jess?"

"I know what you're up to, Alex."

His mouth dried and he stared back at her,

waiting for her to say she had somehow found out who he really was. He wasn't ready to tell her yet.

Tomorrow maybe, after he saw Bartholomew.

"Caught me out, how?"

"Why did you lie about there being no rooms? If you wanted to get in my pants, you didn't have to go to anywhere near the trouble you did. I'm the easy Yank, remember?"

He reached across the table to take her hand, but she snatched it away.

"Don't say that about yourself, Jess."

"In the afternoon, when I come back from the tour, I'm getting a room. One of the *many* vacant rooms tonight," she said.

"Jess, I can explain."

"Pah." She pushed her chair back. "No more lies. Thanks for the lift, Alex. Have a nice life."

Her skirt swirled around her calves as she walked to her room, her back ramrod straight, and then she slammed the door.

Alex dropped his head into his hands and groaned. Maybe it was for the best, but he hated the thought that he'd hurt her. The look in her eyes when she'd called herself the easy Yank tore at his heart. He had to make this right.

Chapter Fifteen

Jess slept poorly with one ear open to listen for Alex leaving, her mind churning, full of her plans for the day. Rolling over, she thumped the pillow and lay still for a minute before giving up on getting back to sleep.

Dawn was about to break. The first glimmers of pink light were tingeing the edges of the dark sky through the window. The back door closed and she heard Alex call to Bowser, and a couple of minutes later the pickup roared to life. The headlights shone on her window as the truck headed past the back of the cabin. Fighting the tears that clogged her throat, she squeezed her eyes shut. It was time she took control.

Crawling out of bed, she dug through her clothes looking for something suitable to wear back out into the outback. This time, she knew what to expect. The only thing she didn't have was a decent pair of boots.

By seven o'clock, she was showered and dressed, and her packed bags were lined up against the back door. She still hadn't decided how long she was going to stay at Cockatoo Springs. It all depended on what today brought. She sipped the coffee she'd brewed. For all she knew, Ricardo could be there already, or if he wasn't there yet, he would be here soon. You couldn't believe one word that came out of Alex's mouth, and besides Monica had said Ricardo *was* here having a meeting with Larry Bartholomew of all people.

Jess stepped out onto the back porch to wait for the tour bus. The sun was already burning hot, so she stepped back into the shade. The heat shimmered over the red sandstone cliffs in the distance. All was still and quiet, and Jess smiled as she glanced across at the lush lawn.

Talk about gullible. She'd believed every word Alex had said and had expected to see saltwater crocodiles roaming around. You'd think a journalist would be savvier. *Sucked in by bedroom eyes and a sexy smile.*

Well, today was a new day and as soon as she finished the bush tucker tour, and got some information for her article, she'd check into the resort and enjoy a few days there before flying home to the North American winter. If Ricardo was here and she did manage to snag some time with him—well, that would be a bonus.

The sound of an engine reached her, and for a moment her heart picked up a beat. She stepped to the front of the porch and grasped the low railing, peering up the road. But it wasn't the pick-up. A high vehicle emblazoned with Cockatoo Springs Tours on the side trundled up the narrow roadway and pulled on to the lawn across from the cabin. Jess turned and lifted her bags out. Hopefully, Alex would still be off fishing, or crabbing or wrestling crocodiles for a while yet.

"Morning, love." The wide smile of the Aboriginal bus driver greeted her. "You're the last one on."

"Is it okay if you drop me back to the resort after the tour? Do you have room for my bags?"

"Not a problem."

First hurdle overcome.

The bus had one empty seat at the very front. Jess tucked her small bag under the seat and sat down, and reached for her seatbelt.

"Whoa, love. Do you have closed in shoes in your suitcase?"

Jess looked down at her leather sandals. They were the most substantial footwear she had with her, apart from the closed in stilettos she'd worn with her suit on the trip over.

"No, this is all I have."

"You can't get off the bus at the gathering site unless you've got closed in shoes." The bus driver shrugged. "Sorry, safety regulations."

Jess leaned over and spoke in a low voice. "I don't *have* any other shoes with me."

He shook his head. "You're welcome to come along for the drive and see the sites, but you won't be able to get off the bus when we gather, and I'll have to give you your morning tea on the bus."

Jess chewed her lip. "I'm sorry, I didn't realise. My…er…friend here booked the trip for me."

What to do? She reached over and leaned on the driver's seat.

"I'll change my trip to another day, then." She put on the best persuasive smile she could muster. "Would you have time to give me a ride to reception before you leave?"

"Not a problem." He turned the motor off and picked up his microphone. "Just a slight detour back to the resort, folks, for this beautiful young lady. Have a read of the brochures in your seat pocket. There is a map of our trip up the coast."

"I really appreciate this." She looked out the window in amazement. She'd read up briefly on Cockatoo Springs after the restaurant had won the award in *Cuisine* and she was trying to find more information about Alessandro Ricardo and the unique concept of the bush tucker chef school. But this luxury was beyond her expectations. The bus passed through the gates and around a high rectangular fountain with sandstone edges, which reflected the colours of the cliffs she had noticed in the distance earlier. *Welcome to Cockatoo Springs* was written in large gold letters on the side of the sandstone edge. A water spout cascaded in the centre of the pool, and the flowing water glistened in the morning sun. It reminded her of the pool and the waterfall at the campsite, except this one had cute ducks paddling on the water.

Don't go there. Move on.

It was early and workers swept the leaves up around the water feature. Jess looked on curiously as a man in a white jacket followed a waddling duck and bent down.

"What's he doing?" she asked as she pointed to the man following the ducks.

The driver laughed. "He's got a great job. Duck pooper-scooper." He changed up a gear and the bus climbed a slight incline. The sparkling ocean opened out in front of her.

Low-level villas on the low slope were almost hidden amongst a profusion of palm trees and brightly coloured tropical plants. A series of paths led down to one of the biggest swimming pools she had ever seen. It was hexagonal shaped with wide walkways through the pool.

"How beautiful is that?" she whispered to herself.

The driver pulled up outside a building marked *Reception* and opened the door.

"You haven't been over yet?" he asked.

"Er, no, I stayed at my friend's cabin last

night. I'm checking in today."

Once her bags were unloaded and the concierge had loaded them onto a trolley, the driver climbed back onto the bus and Jess waved.

The automatic doors to the building opened, and she welcomed the blast of cold air from the air-conditioned reception area. Small palm trees filled the interior in large colourful pots on the shining marble floor, and she crossed the room to the desk.

"Good morning," the male receptionist said. "Checking in? I didn't hear the helicopter."

"No, I came by road." Jess reached down into her bag and removed her credit card. "I don't have a booking, but I rang earlier and I was told there were rooms available."

The clerk tapped on the computer and looked up with a smile. "Yes, I can give you a pool room. Your name?"

"Jessica van Lund." She hated using her father's name, but all her bank accounts were in her legal name.

He ran her card through the terminal and handed her a plastic card. "You're in room two over near the beach side of the pool. Would you like to walk over or shall I order you a cart?"

"Oh, I'll walk. I'll explore on the way." It was too soon to do any digging about Ricardo. She'd get settled before she started work. Once she logged onto her computer, she knew there would be a mountain of email to clear, but that could wait.

"I'll send your luggage over. Enjoy your stay with us, Ms. Van Lund."

A burst of noise and activity came from behind her as she turned around. Two toddlers with black ringlets and wide brown eyes ran across the marble floor, chased by a tall man in black jeans and T-shirt.

"Allegra! Luca! Come back here." The toddlers hid behind one of the sofas and giggled.

"Tomas, they're okay. Chill out."

Jess looked with curiosity at the woman with the Scottish accent who walked over to the reception counter. She was tall with a long dark braid, dressed casually in khaki shorts and a T-shirt.

"They've been cooped up in a helicopter and a bus for two hours." The woman turned to Jess with an apologetic smile. "Just watch you don't get ambushed on your way out. They think they are Dora and Diego in the jungle."

The man shrugged and walked over to join his wife. Jess smiled as she watched the children. The father had an Aussie drawl, the mother, a strong Scottish burr and if she wasn't mistaken the children were chattering away in Italian.

The receptionist held his hand out to the man standing next to her and shook it vigorously. Jess reached down to collect her handbag from the counter.

"Tom, great to see you! Can't believe it's been a year since you were here for Alex's birthday last year."

Jess froze and snuck a look at the man beside her.

Yep, she could see the resemblance. Alex's family had arrived.

After Jess got to her room, she stood at the window looking down at the large swimming pool in the centre of the resort. She'd enquired about meeting the chef, but the guy at the reception desk said he wouldn't be in the restaurant until this afternoon. She'd go over and see this Clay guy as soon as he was over there. If she couldn't work there, maybe he'd do an interview and show her around…or at least set up an appointment for one.

Jess bit her lip, trying to ignore the heavy feeling in her chest. Once she'd realised Alex had been lying to her, and she'd lost her temper, things changed. She had to accept he'd been playing with her all along, and as usual she'd been sucked in. For a couple of nights, there'd been a connection between them. It wasn't just sex…or that's what she'd thought.

When will I ever learn?

She brushed the tears away angrily before they could fall. Now that she was here, she'd make the most of it. On the desk beneath the window a glossy covered compendium listed the services provided by the hotel. First stop, the beauty salon to restore her confidence. Second stop, the pool.

Alex could go take a flying leap.

Chapter Sixteen

The hairdresser lifted the black cape off Alex's shoulders with a flourish. *"Voila,* a new man." She ran her fingers along his hairline. "Alex, you have a white mark on your neck where your hair was so long."

Alex stood and brushed the remaining hair from his suit trousers and tucked his shirt in as he looked in the mirror.

Christ, he hated this part of the job.

All dressed up and looking like a businessman did not sit comfortably with him, but it was a necessary evil. This deal was important and it was the last meeting he'd be having as the managing director. As soon as he signed the contract with Bartholomew, he'd go back to the cabin, get changed, and wait for Jess to come back from the tour. By the time his family descended, he would have made his peace with her, and hopefully she'd be happy to move into the villa with him until she went home. There was no reason they couldn't spend some time together before she went back to the States once he explained why he'd not told her the truth. And he'd give her his first ever interview about Cockatoo Springs and the award-winning chef school. But not about him—he wasn't prepared to go that far.

"Thanks, Wendy. I did leave it a bit long this time." He strolled across the salon and looked across at the doorway to the day spa. "Busy day ahead here? I have a friend staying here who'd like a manicure."

"Send her over. We'll fit her in." Wendy raised her eyebrows. "Friend or family? Having friends at your party this year for a change?"

He grinned. "Friend. Family doesn't arrive till the weekend."

Wendy shook her head. "How long have you been out fishing in the outback? It *is* the weekend."

"Shit. What day is it?"

"Friday. Your party is tomorrow night. The staff is looking forward to it." She gave him another smile and nudged his ribs. "Your sister-in-law is booked in for a treatment this afternoon. You do know your secret is out, don't you?"

Alex narrowed his eyes. "What secret?"

"Clay let it slip in the kitchen last night and it went around like wildfire." Her grin got wider. "You have no idea, do you…Alessandro?"

"Oh, shit."

"We've all suspected for ages. Wondered why a simple barramundi fisherman had the luxury villa on the beachfront kept vacant for him."

Okay he's known this would happen one day, but now Jess being on the scene complicated matters. He'd have to get to Jess the instant she got off the tour. He hoped like hell his name wouldn't come up in discussions. Surprisingly, it just didn't seem to matter that much anymore; the only thing that worried him was Jess being upset. His secret was out, the contract was almost over and he needed to get to Jess before she found out through someone else. She was really angry with him, so he didn't think she'd ask about him. But she might try to ask around about Alessandro.

He reached into his pocket and passed Wendy a tip. "Look after my sister-in-law. Which one is booked in today?"

"Lissy."

Alex stepped out onto the covered walkway that crossed the pool. It was the quickest way to the executive suite where Bartholomew was waiting for him. As soon as the contract was signed he'd seek out whoever of his family had arrived and then he'd wait for Jess. If it all worked out to plan, it would be a great weekend.

Larry Bartholomew was dressed casually in white jeans, and a bright yellow T-shirt stretched tightly across his huge paunch. He took Alex's hand in his large beefy grasp and spoke in a booming voice.

"Good to meet you, son." Alex stiffened,

taking an instant dislike to the gregarious American.

"Now before we look at the paperwork, I want to see all around this place. Your man showed me the contract and it looks all fine and dandy, but I want to see what you think makes this place so special. Maybe I could meet the new chef from London? What do you say, boy?"

"Good." Alex headed for the door. The quicker he did the tour, the sooner the paperwork was signed and he could get away from business and find his family before Jess got back. "Come this way. We'll do the kitchens first and then I'll show you the grounds."

Alex strode out, and the big man hurried along behind him, and was huffing by the time they reached the kitchen. A couple of the sous-chefs were filleting barramundi at the big sink under the window.

"Another fresh shipment in?"

"Yes, they came in on the helicopter about an hour ago."

"The helicopter's in already?"

"Yes, they put on three extra trips this morning. Remember, your family are all arriving today for the party tomorrow night."

"Yes." All the more reason to get this tour over and done with. "Clay's not around?"

"No, he went back to Darwin on the chopper to collect some Asian spices he couldn't order through the supplier. He's coming back in the last helicopter after lunch."

Alex turned to Bartholomew. "Clay's not here. You'll have to meet him later. We'll take a quick tour. One of the vehicles should be there so you can see the level of comfort we'll offer your clients."

"Great!" His loud voice echoed through the large kitchen. "Then we'll get this signed and we can have a drink, boy." Larry slapped him on the back, and Alex clenched his jaw, counting to ten silently before he lost his temper and blew the deal. If it hadn't been for Mitch telling him what a great opportunity it was to break into the overseas luxury market, he would have put the skids under this obnoxious guy straight up.

Alex led him across to the pool area, pointing out the unusual bar located in the middle of the water.

"How about a drink, now?" Some sunbathers lying on the pool lounges near the bar looked across as Larry's voice carried loudly across the water. Alex shook his head.

"There's a bar in the executive suite. We'll get the contract signed first."

He turned and stepped onto the path toward the eastern side of the pool. Bartholomew didn't follow, and Alex turned around waiting for the portly guy to catch him up.

"Gotta love hanging around these places, don't ya reckon? Some nice bikinis around."

Alex nodded with a tight smile. "I have another appointment, Larry. If we don't hurry, I'll have to get my assistant to sort the contract signing out."

Larry followed him with a grunt and they walked across the small bridge dividing the pool from the bar. Alex flicked a glance across to the sun lounges and his breath caught in his throat. On the other side of the bar, Jess was lying on a sun lounge on her stomach. Her head was turned away from them on the pillow, and her arms were crossed beneath her head. A tiny red bikini showed way too much skin. Alex grabbed Larry's arm and motioned him to the opposite direction.

"What the hell is she doing there?" he muttered to himself.

Why wasn't she on the bush tucker tour? The last thing he wanted was for her to see him in his suit doing a deal.

Christ, the day was getting more complicated by the minute.

"Sorry? What did you say?" Larry said.

"I just thought you might like to see the gardens and where the day tours go out."

Larry followed him slowly as Alex strode from the pool area to the bottom floor of the building. "I'd rather have that drink."

"You can come back to the pool later," he said tightly. "If you want your tours to come here, we'll do it my way."

"No need to snap my head off. You want this deal or not?" Larry frowned at him and Alex tried to placate him with a smile.

"Sorry, Larry. I've got a lot of meetings ahead of me today. Look, there's a bottle of fifteen-year-old single malt whisky in my office to seal the deal. As soon as we sign on the dotted line, we'll have that drink."

When they reached the end of the corridor, he shoved the office door open and strode across to his desk and picked up the phone.

"Mitch, I need you. Bring the contract in, please. We're ready to sign." He hung the phone up and turned to Larry, gesturing to an armchair.

"Sit down. I'll pour the drinks." Alex crossed to the small bar by the window and reached for the whisky. He leaned forward as a flash of red caught his eye. Jess was standing beside the sun lounger knotting a red sarong beneath her breasts. As he watched, she turned and headed along the path and disappeared between the trees.

As soon as Mitch arrived and the contract was signed, he was going to track her down and find out what she was doing here. She should be safely up in the gorge collecting bush tucker by now.

He glanced up as Mitch opened the door, and Larry held his hand out.

"I'll have mine neat," Larry said.

"One for me too, please boss," Mitch said. He raised his eyebrows when Alex shoved a glass toward him slopping the whisky on his fingers.

"Mitch." Alex tried to focus on the business at hand, but all he could think of was Jess and wondering if she was heading back to the cabin. "When we finish here, I have another meeting. Can you show Larry around, please?"

"No problem." He shot Alex a curious glance as he held his hand out for the contract. Pulling a pen from his pocket, Alex signed with a flourish and put the contract on the table in front of Larry.

"I may see you around later today, Larry. A pleasure doing business with you." He shook the man's hand briefly and headed for the door.

"Mitch, I'll be out for a while."

He dashed over to his beachfront villa, keeping an eye out for Jess in case she'd come back to the pool, but there was no sign of her. He threw his suit jacket on the sofa. After pulling his tie loose, he unbuttoned his shirt with one hand and dialled reception with the other.

"It's Alex. Have we got a guest by the name of Trent booked in yet?"

He tucked the phone beneath his chin and

stepped out of his suit trousers while he waited for the receptionist to check.

"No guest checked in or booked ahead by the name of Trent. Are you expecting a guest, sir?"

"No, that's fine. Thanks." Alex hung up and let out his breath slowly, relieved Jess was still over at the cabin. She must have wandered over for a swim. Maybe she'd calmed down and they could talk. He'd head straight over there now. It looked like he was going to have to own up to his deception. If the word had gone around about him being Alessandro, he wanted her to hear it from him and no one else.

"Shit," he muttered beneath his breath as he pulled his jeans on. "How did everything get so complicated so quickly? Why does how she feels bother me so much?" Next week couldn't come soon enough. Handing over the management to Mitch and spending the summer fishing was looking very appealing. And then when the season was over, he had some big decisions to make. Was he going to stick around the Territory, or go back south and find a law firm? Or he could travel to the States and look up Jess, if she was still talking to him.

Alex headed to the resort through the pool area in case Jess had come back, but there was no sign of her. It was almost lunchtime and the sun loungers were empty. He nodded to the barman who was filling ice buckets in preparation for the usual after lunch rush to the pool.

"Alex!" For a moment he thought it was Jess and he turned around slowly, but grinned when he saw the woman with a riot of curls running across the pool bridge toward him.

"Lissy!" He lifted her up when she reached him and twirled her around. When he set her down, she hugged him close.

"Alex, it's so good to see you."

He held her hands and looked at her. "So do you, Lissy. Where's my big brother and that nephew of mine?"

"We're up in the lagoon wing next to your parents. They've arrived too. And Tom and Brianna and the twins are on the other side of us." Lissy raised her hand and held his chin and scrutinised him. "Look at you, all tanned and fit. This place has certainly agreed with you. You look a lot better than you did last year."

Alex leaned forward and dropped a light kiss on her forehead. "It's been a good year, Lis. I'm ready to move on."

He looped his arm around her shoulder and turned her in the direction sof the bridge. "I'll take you back to your room and say a quick hello to the family."

He looked around, keeping an eye out for Jess. "I've just got something I have to do before I can settle in and catch up on all the family news."

"I thought you'd handed most of the work over to Mitch."

"Yes, I have. It's something personal. I'll fill you all in later if it works out.

"If it doesn't, I might crack the whisky open."

Alex smiled wryly as they stopped in the middle of the small bridge and exchanged a glance as they both remembered the last time the Richards' brothers had shared a bottle of whisky. It had been the day of Emily's funeral. Lissy looked up at him and her hers filled with tears.

"So you're really okay?"

Alex used his thumb to wipe away the tear that rolled down Lissy's cheek. His sister-in-law was a rock when Emily was killed, and he'd gotten to know her well. He'd never let on to any of his family that Emily had deceived him.

"Yes, I'm really okay. I've moved on, Lis."

Chapter Seventeen

"Damn you," Jess said under her breath. "Damn you, Alex."

She stood at the side of the large window overlooking the pool. She bit the side of her cheek to force away the tears that were threatening to fall. When she saw Alex head toward the pool her heartbeat kicked up, and she'd stood watching him stride across past the pool bar. She decided to act maturely and tell him she was in the resort and was about to turn to head to the door. And let him explain what he'd been up to, because she had known there was something.

When the woman ran across to the bridge to him and Alex took her in his arms and kissed her, Jess's world shattered and she realised what he was hiding. A searing shaft of jealousy engulfed her, and she slid down on to the sofa in front of the window.

She'd been right all along. He'd wanted her in the cabin because he already had someone here at the resort. She would bunker down in her room until she could get the first flight out of here. Stuff the interview and stuff the job.

An ache began in the middle of her chest

and moved up to her throat. For a few minutes she allowed herself to wallow in self-pity and then the anger kicked in. Why should she give up the entire reason for being here just because a man wooed her into his bed?

***

"I'll be back in a half hour or so, I just have to go to the cabin and see someone." Alex hugged his mother for the second time and grinned over the top of her loose black curls at his two older brothers. Having his family here made him all the more determined to make his peace with Jess.

He'd make her see reason. It would be fun to have her at his birthday dinner and he was looking forward to introducing her to his family. He just had to convince her she could trust him.

Nick slapped him on the shoulder as he walked to the door.

"Good to see you looking fit and well, mate. Lissy says you're moving on next week?"

"Yes, contract's up and the school is established and going really well. I've made a few enquiries down in Brisbane, but I was thinking about taking a trip to the States first. I'll tell you about it later over a drink."

He closed the door and left his family, grinning at the noise that came through the door. It was just like the noise that always filled his parent's home when everyone was visiting. Once his sisters arrived with their families, the resort wouldn't know what had hit it.

The door to the cabin was closed and he pushed it open slowly.

"Jess? Jess, are you there?" He checked each room, but there was no sign of her or her belongings.

"Where is she, little buddy?" Alex reached down and scratched the little dog's back. "I wonder where she went." Picking up the phone, he dialled reception. "Has a Ms. Trent registered yet?"

When the clerk said no, Alex began to worry. He called the helicopter office.

"Bill, it's Alex. Have you taken any passengers out this morning?"

"No, mate, I'm just about to fly to Darwin to pick Clay up. I've got an empty bird. Had no one go out so far today. Just incoming guests."

Worry pinched at his gut. Surely, she wouldn't have tried to get out another way.

Where was she?

He picked the phone up again and dialled reception again. "Bill, have you checked in a tall blonde woman this morning?"

"I only just came on duty."

Shit. He ran his hand through his newly cropped hair, surprised to feel the stubble beneath his fingers.

"Can you have a look and tell me if any

female guests have registered this morning by themselves and get me their room numbers."

He stood at the door looking at the sofa, remembering the feel of Jess's smooth skin beneath his hands last night.

"Three, Alex."

"O'Reilly, Van Lund, and Petersen. Rooms 114, 115, and 231." Bill laughed. "Not sure if their blondes or brunettes. Does she have to be a blonde?"

"Very funny."

Giving Bowser a quick pat, he headed back to the resort where he headed to the gift shop. He bought three small gift baskets and made his way up to room 114. He knocked on the door, waited, but there was no reply. He knocked again and waited for a few moments before knocking on 115.

"Just a moment," an unfamiliar voice with a British accent called out.

A petite dark-haired girl opened the door and a taller redhead peered over her shoulder. Alex cleared his throat and handed them one of the baskets. "Good morning. A welcome gift from management. Is one of you in 114?" He presumed the pair of them may be travelling together and have side-by-side rooms.

The redhead piped up. "Yes, I'm in 114."

Alec handed over the second basket of chocolate and flowers, before crossing to the lift and going to the second floor. He tapped lightly on the door of room 231, one of the larger rooms that overlooked the pool.

"Who is it?"

Alex sagged with relief when Jess's voice came through the door.

"A delivery."

"I'm not expecting a delivery."

"Open the door, Jess."

"Why?"

"Because I want to talk to you."

"We have nothing to talk about."

"Please, Jess." Alex put the basket on the floor, prepared to wait her out.

The door opened slowly and Jess peered around the edge. His stomach dropped when he saw her face.

"What do you want?" Her eyes were red, and he was sure she'd been crying.

"I want to talk to you. He reached down for the basket and held it out to her. "Peace offering?"

"Thank you, now go away and leave me alone." She took the basket and began to shut the door. Alex jammed his foot in the space and received an icy glare in return.

"While you're here, you can answer me one question?" she said.

"Yes?"

"Does the job in the kitchen still stand? I

might as well get something out of this awful trip."

"Do you want to?"

"Of course I do."

"Can I come in? Please? We can talk about it."

"No."

Alex sensed he wasn't going to get anywhere by persisting. "Grab me a pen and a piece of paper."

Jess closed the door and for a moment he wondered if she would come back. Then the door opened again and she passed him a hotel notepad and pen without saying a word. He wrote down Clay's name and the phone extension of the kitchen and handed it back to her. She closed the door in his face and the hollow feeling in his stomach was almost as bad as the loss he'd experienced two years earlier when Emily died.

***

Jess frowned at the mirror when she washed her face. Her eyes were swollen, her face was blotchy, and it really bugged her that Alex had seen her like that.

What was he playing at?

She'd seen him with that woman and had nothing more to say to him. No matter if he wanted to apologise for whatever he'd done, or give her flowers and chocolates. She gritted her teeth. She was immovable and she would not give in and listen to him. Picking up the phone, she dialled the extension he'd given her.

"Clay."

"Hello, Clay, my name is Jess. Alex said I might be able to talk to you about a kitchenhand job?"

"Sure, come on down and see me. I'm in the restaurant now."

"I'm on my way."

"Jess, wait!" She took a step back when a firm hand grabbed her elbow. Larry Bartholomew leaned in to hug her.

"Hello, Larry. I heard you were here."

"Just signed a million-dollar deal with Alessandro Ricardo," he said smugly.

So it's true. Ricardo is here.

Jess felt the first glimmer of excitement as her spirits lifted a tiny bit.

"Your father said I might see you here." Larry kept his hand on her arm and she pulled it out of his grasp.

"My father doesn't know I'm here."

Larry leaned in close to her and tapped his nose. "Yes, he does, and what's more he told me you are after an interview with Ricardo." His alcohol-infused breath wafted in front of her. "But there's no need. Don't waste your time. I know all about it and I've already decided to give the job to one of the other freelance journalists. Seeing you're here, we could have some fun together, and who knows what might happen when the next job comes up."

He reached over and ran his fat hand down her arm. The knowledge that her father was tracking her life and career made her feel sicker than Larry already was, and Jess's vision blurred. She leaned in close to tell him exactly what she thought, lowering her voice as there were several people close by on sun lounges.

"Take your hands off me."

Before she could finish, Larry looked away from her and his voice slurred.

"Ricardo, can I buy you another drink."

Alex held her gaze steadily as her world came crashing down around her.

Alex Richards. Alessandro Ricardo.

The penny dropped. Just one more thing he'd lied about and the biggest betrayal when he knew all along she'd been looking for Ricardo. The whole time, from the very first night they had dinner, he'd lied and pretended to be someone else.

I will never trust another man as long as I live.

Gritting her teeth, she forced herself to relax and turned to Larry with a bright smile.

"It was nice to see you, Larry. Say hello to my father for me." She turned away, ignoring Alex who was speaking quietly to her boss. She stood straight and held Alex's gaze as she walked toward the building. A movement next to her caught her attention and she looked up at a woman with a tumble of black curly hair. She looked familiar, but she didn't know who she was. Jess flicked a tight smile in her direction and turned toward her room. A hand grabbed her shoulder; she stopped and lifted her chin high.

"Take your hand off me." She kept her voice low as the woman watched them.

"Jess, we need to talk. I can explain. I had my reasons."

"No, Alex…Alessandro. There is nothing you could say to explain your lies." The woman behind Alex sat up on her sun lounge, following the exchange with great interest. "I am not a bit interested in what you have to say to me. You are a scheming liar, through and through."

He grabbed her arm again. "Jess, there's a lot of stuff I need to tell you. I am not going to let you go while you are so upset.

"Upset." Her voice rose. "You think this is upset. Buddy, you ain't seen nothing yet." She clenched her jaw and glared at him. "Now take your fingers off my arm before I *show* you how upset I can get."

She shook his hand off and strode down the path straight to the reception building. Find the first helicopter out of here and she was on it. There was no way she could look at that man—Alex, Alessandro whatever he decided to call himself—without choking him.

He'd played her for a fool and this easy Yank had fallen right into his arms more than once. Hooked and reeled in like one of his smelly fish and she'd fallen for it, wide-eyed and believing.

She threw her room card onto the counter and the clerk looked up at her.

"Sorry, ma'am. I didn't hear you come in.

"I need a seat on the first helicopter out of here." She looked at the young man as he stared at her. "Please."

"I'm sorry, ma'am, they're fully booked today, even with the extra flights. We've had a lot of guests changing over."

Sweat broke out on her forehead despite the air conditioning, and Jess mopped at her brow with shaking fingers.

The clerk clicked the keyboard and looked at the screen. "The first flight out to Darwin is tomorrow afternoon."

"Book me on it, please. Room 231."

***

Alex stood by the pool and watched Jess stride off. She held her head high and almost swaggered along the path, but he'd seen her eyes. Deep, deep hurt filled them and he was filled with remorse. She turned the corner of the building and disappeared from his sight.

How the hell was he going to explain and apologise and convince her he'd been going to come clean this afternoon?

A gentle hand tugged on his arm. "Do you want to tell me how you made that beautiful girl so sad?"

He looked up and shook his head slowly. "Mama, did you see all that?" He held out his arms and his mother hugged him back.

"Yes, I did. Your sisters have arrived and I decided to have some quiet time around the pool. Brianna and Lissy, and your three sisters, are in the day spa and Nick and Tom are over at the playground with the children."

Warmth filled Alex's chest and some of the distress eased. He dropped his chin into Tessa's hair. "Where's Dad?"

"Where do you think?"

"In your room reading some academic tome?"

"You always were clever." Tessa nodded and smiled up at him. "Now tell me about your lady friend. Can I help?"

"Walk with me. I have to get rid of that horrid man." Alex tucked his mother's hand into the crook of his elbow. "I much prefer fishing to business. Next week, I'm out of here. Come to my villa and I'll tell you the whole sad story."

***

Jess sat cross-legged on her bed, peering at her laptop screen, searching for a flight from Darwin to New York. She'd called Monica to tell her she was on the way home, and called the rental car company arranging for the car to be picked up in Daly River. She'd almost had to mortgage her apartment to pay for it. The earliest she could fly out was tomorrow night via Sydney and Los Angeles.

Thirty-four hours.

Which made it a long, long time until she could lock herself in her apartment, get right away from the world, and lick her wounds. She was tempted to write the damn article anyway and expose Alessandro Ricardo as sexy barramundi fisherman Alex Richards, but her ethics wouldn't let her do that, no matter what a lowlife liar he was.

And what was the point anyway? Larry had already given the job to someone else.

The mouse hovered over the booking and she hesitated.

What was she waiting for? Did she really expect him to come knocking on the door and declare his undying love for her? When would she ever learn? All men were users. The whole damn lot of them. *Her father, her ex-fiancé, Larry Bartholomew, and most of all Alex or Alessandro.*

God, she didn't even know who he really

was, or what his real name was.

She almost fell off the bed as a light tap sounded through the door. It was so soft, she wasn't even sure it was at her door. Jumping off the bed, she smoothed down her short dress with shaking hands and wound her hair up, clipping it back. She'd wait. If it was her door, they'd knock again.

Tap, tap.

Then an unfamiliar female voice called her name "'Jess? Are you there?"

Slowly, she opened the door and peered around. The woman who'd smiled at her beside the pool and watched the exchange between her and Alex stood there.

"I know you don't know me." She tipped her head to the side and smiled. "I'm Tessa. Tessa Richards. Can I come in?"

"Tessa Richards?" Jess opened the door and stepped back.

Deep brown eyes lit up in a smile. "I'm Alex's mother."

"Oh." Jess swallowed and wondered why she was here. "So, he is Alex Richards, then."

"I saw how upset you were when you left my son and I wanted to check on you."

It was a long time since anyone apart from Monica had cared about how she was. Her eyes pricked with tears and she couldn't hold back the single tear that rolled down her cheek.

"I'm fine."

Tessa held her arms out. "Oh, sweetheart, you're not."

Jess crumpled and burst into tears. "Why does it always happen to me?"

Tessa smoothed her hair as she sobbed into the shoulder of the mother of the man who had broken her heart. It was surreal—a strange woman comforting her in a way her own mother had never done.

After a couple of minutes, she pulled back. "I'm sorry," she said between hiccoughs. "How embarrassing. You don't even know me."

Tessa went over to the small kitchenette and pointed to the kettle. "May I?"

Jess nodded and sat on the side of the bed while Tessa filled the kettle.

"Tea or coffee?"

"Coffee, please." Jess sat up straight and wiped her eyes, mortified by her show of emotion.

Tessa carried the cups over to the small table by the window, with a jug of milk and sugar bowl. Jess shook her head.

"Just black for me, thanks."

Tessa sat and gestured for her to join her. "I need to tell you a story."

Jess looked at Alex's mother. Jet-black hair without a single strand of grey was held back with a bright red ribbon. Soft wrinkles around her eyes spoke of years of laughter. She stirred her coffee and set the spoon on the saucer.

"I saw the way my son looked at you and I knew straight away you were special to him." Tessa picked up her cup and blew softly on the hot liquid. "Two years ago, I worried if he would ever smile again. Now I have seen him smile, and I know he has found his happiness again."

Jess frowned remembering their conversation about something personal that had been the catalyst for Alex giving up law and moving to the Top End.

"Whatever you have given him, you have broken down the wall he erected around himself. He thought he could protect himself and prevent himself from suffering again."

"What happened?"

"He was engaged to a sweet, sweet girl. He and Emily bought a house in Brisbane where Alex was about to move from his government job and start with a top law firm. She was killed in a mindless accident by a drugged-out truck driver and the grief took control of him. I know there is more, but Alex has never shared it, but I suspect it is why he signed the contract to manage this place for two years."

Jess closed her eyes. She couldn't imagine what Alex had gone through.

"We're a very close family despite being

scattered over the world. But we lost Alex for two years. The only way to stay with him was for us to come up here, and we have a family pledge that we will share his birthday each year, no matter what we are doing."

Jess blinked away the tears that were blurring her vision.

"Jess, this year, my Alex is back. He is alive and full of life for the first time since Emily was killed. I saw the way he looked at you." Tess squeezed her hands. "I beg you to give him a chance."

Jess pulled her hands back and dropped her head. "I can't say I have been through the grief Alex has, but I saw him with another woman." She lifted her gaze to meet Tessa's and her voice caught. "I can't take the risk of trusting my heart again."

"Oh, my dear. Look in the mirror. Look at the expression in your eyes when you talk of him."

Jess covered her face with her hands, shaking her head. "I don't know."

They were quiet for a moment and then the phone rang, breaking the silence. Jess crossed the room and picked it up, her hands shaking.

"Yes?" She listened, disappointment settling deep within her as the voice of the receptionist came over the phone. She listened and nodded, turning away from Tessa's curious gaze.

"Yes, please. I'll be ready. I'll have my bags

ready to collect."

She turned to Alex's mother and couldn't stop the tears spilling from her eyes.

"I'm sorry, Tessa. I need time to think this through. I'm getting picked up in half an hour. There's a spare seat on the last helicopter to Darwin this afternoon."

Tessa stood. "Well, I'd better let you get packed up then." She walked to the door. "I understand you have to do what is right for you. And trust me, he has no other woman. It may have been one of his sisters or sisters-in-law you saw him with."

Jess's vision blurred as the door closed quietly behind the mother of the first man who had truly captured her heart.

Chapter Eighteen

Jess adjusted the headphones over her ears and listened to the bright and breezy voice of the helicopter pilot.

"Welcome, folks, and I hope you've enjoyed your stay at Cockatoo Springs." She leaned her head on the glass and closed her eyes, blocking out the view of the opalescent water below.

The call had come too quickly. She'd made the instant decision to take the ride out and she was regretting it. Now she knew she'd been too harsh when she judged Alex. His reason for keeping his privacy had been his decision to make and he was entitled to put up those barriers. If she was honest, she had done the very same thing, changing her name informally back to Trent. The circumstances that had thrown them together had not been entirely of his doing, and she couldn't blame him for anything that happened since.

In one fleeting moment she knew she could be persuaded. Perhaps she should have listened to what he had to say. Static sounded in her headphones and the pilot spoke.

"The territory is a big place, folks, and if

you look below, you can see one of the magnificent sandstone escarpments that are a feature of this landscape. Take a good look, you won't ever see that one from the ground. The land was formed by…"

Jess switched her attention from the commentary to her problem at hand.

She wouldn't ever see any more of this rugged landscape from the ground or air. Once she was back in New York, she was going to quit her job with Larry and chase all of the freelance articles she could find. Screw Larry Bartholomew and his fixing of jobs. She'd make sure her father couldn't find out every detail of her life. She was going to have that one out with him as soon as she got back to New York.

The helicopter banked sharply to the right and she blanked out his voice. Until the helicopter began to lose height and she paid attention.

"…apologise again for the delay. We have to make a quick trip back to Cockatoo Springs. Nothing to worry about. Just a message from management that has to be dealt with." He turned and grinned at Jess and gave her a thumbs up.

No, it couldn't be.

She fought the tingle of anticipation curling in her stomach.

No, he wouldn't.

The helicopter descended to the helipad, and

she kept her eyes tightly shut. She wasn't going to allow herself to be disappointed. She gripped her hands in her lap and took a deep breath. A light touch on her leg caught her attention and she slowly opened her eyes.

The pilot pointed to her seat belt as the other three passengers looked on curiously. "The boss wants to see you."

Jess looked out the window and the pilot slid the door open.

A tall man with short black hair in a pair of faded denim jeans and a white T-shirt leaned back against a dusty pickup truck. A little brindle dog sat patiently at his feet. Tears pricked her eyes. The pilot took her hand and helped her down the step to the skid. Jess walked slowly over to the truck, her hair blowing across her face in the afternoon breeze.

"Hello, Jess."

"Hello, Alex." She reached up and pushed the strands from her face. "Is that what I call you?"

"That's who I am," he said looking down. "I called the helicopter back because there was a sad dog here that missed you. He was upset because you didn't say goodbye."

Jess looked down at the dog sitting at Alex's feet. "Hey, Bowser."

When she said his name, he jumped up and put his front paws on her knees and she scratched the top of his head. The little staffy stretched his head back and looked at her with adoration in his warm brown eyes. She looked up and warmth filled her from her head to her toes.

"Mine's not the only heart you've captured, Jess," he said softly.

Lifting her hand, she brushed her fingers against his bare neck. "I like you better with long hair and your piece of string."

Alex reached up and placed his hand over hers and held it against his neck. He lowered his forehead to touch hers. "We have a lot of talking to do. I never meant to hurt you."

"I know." His lips hovered over hers while he waited for her to finish speaking. "And I was less than truthful with you."

His breath whispered over her lips and she closed her eyes. The warmth of his mouth took hers in a gentle kiss full of unspoken promise.

They both ignored the cold, wet nose that pushed between their legs. Eventually Bowser gave up and ran across to join the rest of the Richards family who stood outside the gate to Cockatoo Springs.

And there wasn't a crocodile in sight.

Epilogue

Twelve months later

Jess's computer dinged and a message came up on the screen.

Meeting in my office… now.

She logged off and picked up her cardigan from the back of the chair. She was surprised how cold these executive offices could get. And if she knew the boss, it could be a long meeting. He didn't spend much time in his office, but when he did, the meetings went on forever. She opened her office door and smiled at the name plate on the door.

Jess Trent. Senior Executive. Publicity.

It hadn't taken quite the years she'd thought it would, but she'd made it.

An office with her name on the door.

Granted, it was a bit of a detour from where she'd been heading, but the last year had been a stepping stone to bigger things than food journalism. She tapped lightly on the door of the office and was called in. Her boss was sitting in the large leather chair looking out the window at the busy scene below.

"Come in, Jess." He swung the chair around and looked at her. "I have a problem I hope you can help me with."

She looked at him without speaking. He rose from the chair and came around to stand beside her.

"I'm getting the offices refurbished and I don't know what to put on your door."

She frowned and shook her head looking up at him. "What do you mean?"

"Well, the name plate could be Jessica Trent or Jessica Van Lund."
Alex dropped to one knee and pulled a small silver box from his pocket. "Or I'd be much happier if it was Jessica Richards."

Jess gasped and kneeled down beside the man who had given her so much happiness since she had moved to Cockatoo Springs one year ago.

"I think Jessica Richards sounds wonderful."

THE END

Book 1 Nick's story: The Trouble with Paradise

Book 2 Tom's story: Marry in Haste

Visit Annie's website to subscribe to her newsletter to stay up to date with release dates:

Other Books by Annie Seaton

Whitsunday Dawn
Undara
Osprey Reef

Porter Sisters Series
Kakadu Sunset
Daintree
Diamond Sky
Hidden Valley
Larapinta

Pentecost Island Series (2020)
Pippa
Eliza
Nell
Tamsin
Evie
Cherry
Odessa
Sienna
Tess
Isla

Anthologies
Pentecost Island 1-3
Pentecost Island 4-6

Pentecost Island 7-10

Bondi Beach Love Series
Beach House
Beach Music
Beach Walk
Beach Dreams
The House on the Hill Boxed Set

Prickle Creek Series
Her Outback Cowboy
Her Outback Surprise
His Outback Nanny
His Outback Temptation

Second Chance Bay Series
Her Outback Playboy
Her Outback Protector
Her Outback Haven
Her Outback Paradise

Love Across Time Series
Come Back to Me
Follow Me
Finding Home
The Threads that Bind

The Richards Brothers
The Trouble with Paradise
Marry in Haste
Crocodile Springs

Sunshine Coast

Waiting for Ana
The Trouble with Jack
Healing His Heart

Deadly Secrets
Adventures in Time
Silver Valley Witch
The Emerald Necklace
Ten Days in Tuscany
Worth the Wait
Full Circle
Baby It's Hot Outside

About the Author

Annie lives in Australia, on the beautiful north coast of New South Wales. She sits in her writing chair and looks out over the tranquil Pacific Ocean. She writes contemporary romance and loves telling the stories that always have a happily ever after. She lives with her very own hero of many years and they share their home with Toby, the naughtiest dog in the universe, and Barney, the rag doll kitten, who hides when the four grandchildren come to visit.
Stay up to date with her latest releases at her website: http://www.annieseaton.net

If you would like to stay up to date with Annie's releases, subscribe to her newsletter here: http://www.annieseaton.net